Kidsboro

Battle for Control
The Rise and Fall of the Kidsborian Empire
The Creek War
The Risky Reunion

BATTLE FOR CONTROL

by Marshal Younger

from Adventures in Odyssey®

Tyndale House Publishers, Inc.

Carol Stream, Illinois

Battle for Control
Copyright © 2008 by Focus on the Family
All rights reserved. International copyright secured.

A Focus on the Family book published by
Tyndale House Publishers, Inc., Carol Stream, Illinois 60188

Focus on the Family and Adventures in Odyssey and their accompanying logos
and designs are federally registered trademarks, and *Kidsboro* is a trademark of
Focus on the Family, Colorado Springs, CO 80995.

TYNDALE and Tyndale's quill logo are registered trademarks of Tyndale
House Publishers, Inc.

Editor: Kathy Davis
Cover design by Joseph Sapulich
Cover illustration © 2008 by Rob Johnson. All rights reserved.

Library of Congress Cataloging-in-Publication Data
Younger, Marshal.
 Battle for control / Marshal Younger.
    p. cm. — (Kidsboro ; 1) (Adventures in Odyssey)
 Summary: Ryan Cummings, the mayor of Kidsboro, is losing control of
his town, but when a new mayor takes over and things begin to get out
of hand, it is Ryan the citizens depend on to make things right again.
 ISBN-13: 978-1-58997-409-8
 ISBN-10: 1-58997-409-3
 [1. Politics, Practical—Fiction. 2. Conduct of life—Fiction. 3. Christian
life—Fiction.] I. Title.
 PZ7.Y8943Bat 2007
 [Fic]—dc22
                                          2006036540

Printed in the United States of America
1 2 3 4 5 6 7 8 9 /13 12 11 10 09 08

*To Stephanie, who worked so hard to
keep a roof over our heads
while I sat at a computer and wrote
a bunch of stuff that will never sell
(and a couple of things that did).*

● ● ●

THE BIRTH OF A CITY

CAREER DAY WAS A BUST. There were tables lined up end-to-end across the Odyssey Middle School gym, and as soon as our teachers let us loose, we all dashed around like 300 mice scrambling for six pieces of cheese, eager to sign up for the fun jobs. If we signed our names on the list fast enough, we had a good chance of working in whatever occupations we wanted for a day. Most everyone wanted exciting things like working at the fire department or police station. At one point, I saw Alice Funderburk, a rather large girl, shove people out of the way as she steamrolled to the police station table. The crowd of people parted for her like the Red Sea. She was the first one to sign up.

I didn't worry too much about getting on the list quickly, because I figured there weren't too many people interested in what I was interested in—politics. I wanted to be the mayor. I wanted so badly to meet with, work with, and *think* with the mayor of Odyssey. I strolled casually to my table, all the while watching people clamor and fight for their own tables, and sure enough, when I got there, no one had signed the sheet. I signed my name, *Ryan Cummings, age 12.* I could hardly wait to walk up the City Hall steps in the only suit I owned, ready to dazzle the mayor of Odyssey with my knowledge of government and politics.

It was not worth the wait.

When I got to City Hall later that morning, the mayor wasn't even around. The secretary showed me his office, and I sat at his desk. There were stacks of papers in front of me that I wasn't allowed to look through. I tried to answer the phone once and I got yelled at. I just sat there and waited for three hours, and when I finally met him, he shook my hand, had a picture taken of the two of us, and told me he was very sorry but he had a meeting to attend. I was dismissed shortly afterward. If all I had wanted was a photo, I could've posed with the cardboard cutout of himself that he still had in his office from his election campaign. I was bitterly disappointed. I wanted to work with him. I wanted to, for a few moments, *be* the mayor.

When I went to Whit's End that afternoon, I found some comfort in the fact that my friends had much the same experience I'd had. We all sat at the counter of the ice cream shop, complaining about our day. John Avery Whittaker, or "Whit" as most adults called him, was the owner and operator of the ice cream shop and discovery emporium and had the misfortune of having to listen to us whine.

Jill Segler had gone to the *Odyssey Times* to find out what it was really like to be a news reporter. She'd had dreams of uncovering some big business scandal.

"I went to Dale Jacobs's office," she began, knowing

everyone would recognize the name of the editor of the *Odyssey Times*, "and the first thing he tells me is, 'It may be a slow news day.' Come to find out, it was not a slow news day. It was a *no* news day. I ended up helping a guy write a story about how celery prices have risen 5 percent in the last two weeks."

Mr. Whittaker chuckled.

Scott Sanchez, my best friend, had a similar experience. He had signed up to learn how to be a private detective. Unfortunately, his mentor was Harlow Doyle, a private eye in Odyssey who may have actually been a worse detective than Scott was.

"We spent two hours filling out my paperwork. All he had to do was sign the form to prove that I showed up. First he couldn't find a pen, then he couldn't decide whether he should sign his middle name, then he couldn't remember his middle name, and then he confused my name with his own. It was unbelievable."

Alice Funderburk also had a frustrating story. She was angry that they didn't give her a gun when she checked in at the police station. She spent most of the morning riding around with a police officer and handing out parking tickets. But when Alice threw a jaywalker up against a wall, she was forced to go back to the police station and do paperwork for the rest of the day.

The only person who had a positive story was Nelson Swanson, who worked with Eugene Meltsner, an employee at Whit's End. Eugene was the resident genius, and Nelson was his protégé. Eugene had helped Nelson conceive and build some of his best inventions, of which he had many. Eugene and Nelson had spent the day building a solar-powered air conditioner. Everyone felt sorry for Nelson when he told this story—until we realized that he had actually enjoyed doing it.

We all whined some more. I said, "How are we ever going to know if this is what we really want to do with our lives if we never get a real opportunity to try it?"

Mr. Whittaker didn't answer. Instead, he began to stare at nothing, which made us think that the wheels were turning inside his head.

"Mr. Whittaker?" Scott said, waving a hand in front of his face.

"You know what?" He said, breaking out of his trance. "If you really want practical experience at these jobs, there may be other ways of getting it."

"How?"

"Why don't you create your own jobs?"

None of us knew what he was talking about, and maybe he didn't either, because he paused and stared into space again. "Better yet . . . why don't you create your own *town*?"

Still, we weren't getting it. "I'll get you started," he said. "You can form a community. Each of you would have a different job—whatever you want to be. It won't be exactly the same as real life, but it might give you a taste of what you're looking for."

I nodded more and more as he went on explaining his idea. I loved it! We could create our own town!

• • •

And so Kidsboro was born. We started off with five of us: Jill Segler would start the *Kidsboro Chronicle*, a weekly newspaper. Alice Funderburk chose to be the chief of police. She had no police to be chief *of*, but no one was about to argue with her. Nelson wanted to be a small-business owner, selling his inventions. Scott wanted to be a private detective, though I couldn't imagine what kinds of cases he would be called on to solve in a town of, presently, five. And none of us were criminals.

Me? I wanted to be the mayor . . . and no one had any objections. The others seemed to think I was the perfect choice, and this made me feel good. I liked my title—mayor of Kidsboro.

The five of us became the city council, and with Mr. Whittaker's help, we wrote the city charter, or the Kidsboro Constitution. All the laws of the land would be laid down in this document.

After we wrote the city charter, we decided that if we were going to do this, we would do it right. "I think we should have actual buildings," I said in our first city council meeting.

"What do you mean?" Jill asked.

"Mr. Whittaker owns the woods behind Whit's End, and he told me we can use it. I think we should build clubhouses for our offices and bigger clubhouses for meeting halls."

"Build clubhouses?" Scott said. "With what?"

This question led us to another question. Was our new

town going to be just the five of us, or would we allow other people in? The clubhouse question answered this for us, because we ran into an immediate problem: none of us had any kind of building materials. Mr. Whittaker didn't want to supply our materials, because he wanted us to come up with our own solutions.

We all knew someone who had a supply of wood, and admitting him as a citizen would solve our problem. Max Darby's father owned a construction company, and Max had easy access to wood scraps. I was worried about asking Max to be a part of Kidsboro, though, because he was known for getting into trouble at school. But having him as a citizen would make it easy for us to get the wood we needed to build our town.

We asked Max, and he loved the idea of becoming a citizen because he thought it could make him rich. He would make us pay for the wood. That's when we decided to set up a money system for Kidsboro. Max would get Kidsboro money (instead of real money) for his wood: tokens (about five cents) and starbills (20 tokens, or about a dollar).

Everything sold in Kidsboro would have to be paid for in Kidsboro money. Mr. Whittaker decided that everyone who became a citizen would be given a certain amount of Kidsboro currency to start off with: enough to buy a house and have a little money left over to spend around town.

Over the next couple of weeks, with Max's help, we built a clubhouse for each of us. Eugene Meltsner was closely involved with the layout of the town, making logical decisions about where everything should go based on proximity to neighbors, quality of soil, and drainage. We also built a meeting hall, which was an open-air pavilion 10 times as large as any of the clubhouses. It was a multi-purpose city council meeting hall and entertainment center.

The next step was to build up our population. We began a search for citizens. Everyone we talked to seemed excited about the idea of being part of a kids' town, so we didn't have much difficulty finding interested people. Everyone was welcome to come to Kidsboro, but it was simply impossible to allow everyone to become actual citizens. We couldn't build that many clubhouses.

We decided that the requirements for citizenship in Kidsboro should be high. We wanted people of reasonably high standards so that we could build up a strong community. The city council would vote on each candidate. I disagreed with a couple of the selections: Valerie Swanson, for one. She was Nelson's sister and a very manipulative girl. But she was voted in despite my arguments against her. That's because she was the prettiest and most popular girl in school. I knew that most of the guys at Odyssey Middle School had secret crushes on her.

Mr. Whittaker gave us advice whenever we really needed it, but for the most part, he held back. He wanted us to get the experience of solving our own problems, and I appreciated this. I doubted that I would ever go to him for advice on a mayoral problem, but I knew that I could if I needed to.

So we had our little town. We started off with 20 people and added more over the next couple of months. Things went smoothly at first. Most Kidsboro citizens came to the town after school through the early spring months, and a lot of us spent our weekend days there. People obeyed the laws; businesses were set up and seemed to be prospering. And I was the mayor.

Which also made me the prime target.

ONE

THE PIT BULL AT MY DESK

MY FOOT SEEMED TO HAVE a life of its own as it tapped uncontrollably on the ground. I pressed it flatter against the ground in an attempt to stop it, but I couldn't. Fortunately for me, the desk hid my foot's nervous dance from Valerie. I've heard that in the presence of vicious animals, you should never show fear, because it's the first thing they sense. I forced myself to look at her, stone-faced. She would not see me flinch.

She spoke, an evil smile crossing her otherwise perfect face. "I don't care if you *are* the mayor, Ryan. If I don't get what I want, I'm gonna take over this town and run you out."

I felt the blood drain out of my face. I tried to return the smile, even though I knew that was silly. Valerie's smile didn't convey friendship or kindness. The fact that Valerie smiled was worse than if she had frowned or gritted her teeth. A frown would've meant she was serious about crushing me into tiny little bits. A smile meant she would also enjoy it.

She stood up without taking her eyes off of me. She leaned over my desk until her long, brown hair was almost swinging in my face. It smelled like strawberries, and for a split-second I was distracted. But I shook off the momentary crush and stared at her eyes, which were half-closed like a lion ready to pounce.

"Ashley gets in," she said. She turned around and left, her work here done.

Whew! I could finally exhale. I wiped the sweat from my forehead with a sleeve and paced around the office, trying to work off some nervous energy. Most of the guys in our school, including me, actually admitted to being afraid of Valerie. The guys who wouldn't admit it were lying. And crushing me under her cruel thumb would be as easy for Valerie as crushing an ant with her foot.

We had grown to 29 citizens in our short two-month history, and we were planning to accept a new person into our town to make it an even 30. That afternoon, Valerie's best friend, Ashley, would be reviewed by the city council for possible citizenship. Valerie was trying to ensure that Ashley got the votes required to get in. One thing about Valerie: It was horrible being her enemy, but it was great being her friend. Having power in your corner has many advantages. Valerie knew that the five council members had to vote on Ashley. If Ashley didn't get an 80 percent majority vote (meaning four out of five people had to say "yes"), she didn't get in at all. No doubt Valerie pretty much knew how the voting would go: Ashley had three votes in the bag, and one vote against her. I was the wild card. If I voted yes to Ashley, she got in. If I voted no, she didn't.

The problem was, I didn't like Ashley. She called me

"Dummings," a less-than-clever variation of my last name, Cummings, plus she got into trouble a lot in school. I'd seen her cheat on tests and copy other people's homework assignments. She was not the type of person I wanted in my town. Kidsboro was a community filled with good citizens who followed rules. After all, this was not a real city—we couldn't actually force anyone to pay a fine or stay in jail, so everyone had to follow the rules on his or her own. A person like Ashley wouldn't take the laws seriously. I was sure of that.

So here was my choice: I could put the town in danger by allowing in a person who might ruin it; or I could put *myself* in danger by tugging on the chain of a fierce pit bull named Valerie.

Politics.

●　●　●

I went to the meeting hall pavilion where the city council met. All five members of the council gathered around the table.

Scott Sanchez was talking to himself, muttering the phrase "Walk the dog" over and over, which most likely meant that he was supposed to go home and do that right after the meeting. He would probably end up forgetting anyway, as he usually did.

To Scott's left, *Kidsboro Chronicle* reporter Jill Segler had her notebook out and a pencil resting on her ear. Next to her, Police Chief Alice Funderburk was jerking her head back and forth to crack the bones in her thick neck.

Finally, Nelson Swanson was studying a chart he had created on his computer. At the top, the heading was "Voting for

Ashley." Below the heading were two columns—a list of reasons for voting "yes" and a list of reasons for voting "no." In the "no" column were all the things that I would've had in *my* "no" column—that Ashley was not very nice, that she was a dishonest student, and so on. In the "yes" column was one phrase, typed in the biggest font Nelson could fit on the sheet of paper: "VALERIE WON'T KILL ME!" Nelson was Valerie's brother and the only one smarter than her in town. But unlike her, he used his intelligence in positive ways.

They sat there staring at me, knowing exactly what was going through my head. Ashley's future in Kidsboro, and possibly *my* future as a living, walking human being, depended on my vote. Jill and Alice would vote for Ashley because she always invited them to her birthday parties. Ashley lived on Trickle Lake and her birthday party always included boating, swimming, and water skiing. It was the best party of the year. So Jill and Alice would vote for her simply because they wanted that invitation in their mailboxes.

Nelson would end up voting for Ashley. Getting Valerie mad at *me* was one thing. But actually living with her every day in adjoining rooms like he did, where she had easy 24-hour access to his neck, would be a nightmare.

I knew Scott would vote against Ashley. Scott had never liked Ashley, and he would do anything to keep her out, even if it meant putting his life in danger.

So the vote would be three to one. If I voted yes, the vote would be four to one, and Ashley would have the required 80 percent.

We went around the room. "Yes," Alice said.

"Yes," Jill said.

"No," Scott said.

"Yes," Nelson said.

No surprises. They all sat up in their chairs and gazed at me. I could almost feel Valerie's hands around my neck, ready to squeeze. I took a long breath, still not quite sure what I was going to say. I closed my eyes tightly. Sweat began to drip down my face. Not a sound came from the other four members of the council as I opened my eyes and let the word slide off my tongue.

"No."

TWO

DANGEROUS CHOICES

I REMAINED SEATED AS EVERYONE filed out of the meeting hall past me. Nelson looked at me the way a priest would look at a man who was about to be executed. He adjusted his glasses and put his hand on my shoulder as if to say, "Bless you, my son," and that he'd pray for my soul. Scott, being my best friend, probably thought he should be supportive, and so he said, "The town thanks you." Then he went to his clubhouse, obviously forgetting that he was supposed to go walk the dog. Jill smiled as if she just might have a homicide to report in the next edition of the newspaper. Alice offered her protection. I think she was joking, but I'm not sure.

As I left the meeting hall, I expected Valerie to jump around the corner immediately, but she didn't. This frightened me. I figured I would be okay as long as I could look her in the eye. But if she lurked in the shadows, I'd probably go nuts. Maybe she knew this. Maybe her plan was to drive me crazy by *not* acting. It would certainly cause everyone in town to wonder whether they should have a mayor who was insane. Then, when she had everyone thinking I should be locked up, she would take over. That was probably her plan . . . and it was working rather well so far.

● ● ●

My stomach was in knots, so I walked to Whit's End to get something to drink.

"Hello, Ryan," Mr. Whittaker said from behind the counter.

"Hi, Mr. Whittaker."

"Is something wrong?" he asked.

"Why?"

"You look a little pale."

"My stomach hurts."

"Are you sick?"

"No," I said, "but I may be dying."

"What?"

He made me sit down and spill the whole story of Valerie and Ashley and the city council vote. He smiled and said, "You made the right choice, even though it could make things difficult for you. I wish *all* of our political leaders had your standard of ethics. So, who are you going to nominate next?"

I hadn't thought about that. Since Ashley didn't get in, I had to come up with a new candidate for citizenship. I had a few ideas off the top of my head.

"I've been thinking about Larry Mankowicz." He was a track star at Odyssey Middle School—a very popular guy who would put Kidsboro on the map just by being there. "Also, Mary Burgess," I said. Mary was the second prettiest girl in our school, in my opinion, next to Valerie.

"Oh . . . okay," Mr. Whittaker said, bowing his head and suddenly becoming very interested in cleaning a glass. He knew both of these people, and though he didn't say it, I could tell he disapproved of my choices. I saw him glance over to one of the booths, and I followed his look. Sitting in the corner by himself was Roberto Santana. I barely knew him, though I knew he had moved to Odyssey from the Dominican Republic about two years earlier. He didn't appear to have many friends. I knew what Mr. Whittaker wanted me to do, though he refused to say it. I felt a little ashamed. I was picking people based on what they could do for Kidsboro, not for what Kidsboro could do for them.

"I catch your drift," I told Mr. Whittaker.

"What?" he said innocently.

I smiled and left. I had to get council approval.

● ● ●

"There he is," I said to Scott as we ate lunch in the school cafeteria. I pointed to Roberto, sitting alone at the very last table. He was eating at lightning speed so he could run to the library, where he could be by himself and not have everybody staring at the kid who was sitting alone. He did that every day.

"Roberto Santana?" Scott asked. "Are you sure?"

"He's perfect," I said.

Scott dipped a French fry into his ketchup. "Excuse me for bringing this up, but you do know his dad's in jail, right?"

"That's just a rumor." I hated the way kids believed anything they heard. The latest gossip was that Roberto's dad was in jail. No one knew exactly why, but everyone had a guess. Roberto denied all of it. I believed him, though I had no evidence on my side either.

"Maybe it's a rumor, maybe it isn't," Scott said.

"Yeah, but even if it is true, which I doubt, why should that matter?"

Scott shrugged, his ketchup-soaked French fry dangling limply from his hand. "We don't want any trouble in our town, do we?"

"What Roberto does and what his father may or may not have done are two different things."

"So maybe we should ask him," Scott said.

"Ask him if his father's in jail?"

"Yeah. The city council's gonna want to know."

"Why should it matter?" I asked.

"I don't know. You don't think it matters?"

"No."

Family matters were private. I knew this especially, because I wanted my own family matters to be private. My mother and I had moved from California to Odyssey when I was eight. No one knew anything about my life before I came to Odyssey, and I was determined to keep it that way. It was something I never talked about, even with Scott. Roberto had a right to keep his mouth shut too.

"Pardon me for breathing," Scott said, "but does he even wanna be in Kidsboro?"

"I told him about it," I said, "and he seemed to think it was a cool idea."

• • •

The next day I presented Roberto's name to the city council. I was met with a less-than-enthusiastic response.

"Do you really know him?" Jill asked.

"No. But I know he's smart. He got the best grade in my history class."

"How is knowing history going to help us?" Scott asked, still not convinced of Roberto's worth.

"I don't think he knows how to speak English," Alice said.

"Yes he does."

"I'm just trying to figure out how he's going to help Kidsboro," Jill said.

"We didn't ask that question about any other candidate. I mean . . . we've got people in this town who have almost no positive qualities at all except that they're somebody's friends. Now why does Roberto have to live up to higher expectations?"

They all exchanged looks.

Nelson was the only one brave enough to speak up. "I know this may not be a reason to keep him out, but you do know about his dad—"

"Yes!" I answered angrily. "I know what people say about his dad. What does that have to do with *him*?"

Nelson adjusted his glasses. "Some studies indicate that criminal behavior is genetic."

"Have any of you ever seen Roberto steal anything?" I asked.

They shook their heads.

"Have any of you ever seen him destroying property? Getting into a fight?" More heads shaking. "Then we have no evidence that he is anything but a good student. *That* we have evidence for."

"I agree," Jill said. "We can't keep him out because of his father. But I think he should have a probation period. A couple of weeks to show us what he's got—since nobody really even knows him."

Everybody around me nodded. I was against this, but I was confident that Roberto would soon show everyone that he could be an asset to the community. So I agreed. Roberto would become a citizen of Kidsboro, but he would be watched very closely.

I gave Roberto the news (though I didn't mention the probation), and he seemed happy about it. I had a feeling he was just thrilled to be a part of something.

● ● ●

Scott and I showed Roberto around the town, including his new clubhouse. Usually, new citizens were given a plot of land, and then they were responsible for buying the wood to build their own houses. But our town builder and handyman, Nick, had built this one for Jeffrey, a boy who had come in about two weeks before, but had moved away suddenly. We gave Roberto the choice of buying this clubhouse or building his own. He decided this one was fine. It was just like everybody else's anyway. It was a rectangular box made of scrap wood that was big enough to stand up in, with about a foot and a half of head room for most people. If you stretched out both arms, you could touch either wall at its width, and its length was enough for two people to lay end-to-end. You had to duck your head to get through the door.

"Very nice," he said, and we exchanged smiles.

Then we showed him the business district—the newspaper office, the church, the police station, and the bakery. We saved the bakery for last because it was the most successful business in Kidsboro.

We turned the corner around the meeting hall and saw the sign for Sid's Bakery. Sid, one of two African-Americans in Kidsboro, made muffins, donuts, cookies, and cakes—all himself. He used ingredients that he bought from Mr. Whittaker. We could all buy smaller items from Mr. Whittaker with tokens, and he would buy ingredients or parts from the store with real money. Obviously, this meant Mr. Whittaker would be spending his own money and getting nothing in return since he couldn't use the tokens anywhere but Kidsboro, but this was one of the sacrifices he made in order to keep Kidsboro going.

Sid's business had thrived. He had one advantage in that kids are never too picky about freshness, so he could frequently sell a three-day-old donut. The bakery was not much bigger than a regular clubhouse, but Sid always had a table full of pastries inside. I hadn't been there in a while, and I thought I would buy a cinnamon-raisin donut for Roberto as a "Welcome to Kidsboro" gesture. But when we got there, Sid was leaving.

"Where are you going?" I asked.

"You're too late. I just threw away my last donut," Sid said. Roberto was visibly disappointed.

"You're closing already?"

"Yep. Forever." Sure enough, there on the outside of the door was a sign that read "Going Out of Business Sale." Sid closed the door behind him. "We had muffins for a token apiece," he said. "You should've been here."

Sid's muffins were usually four tokens each—and everyone in Kidsboro would agree that they were worth it. Most people in town had some vague idea about what they wanted to be when they grew up. Sid didn't just have an idea. He had a destiny. At age 13, he was a fine chef in the making. He was already better than my mom—not that my mom was a bad cook. He was just a master—a pastry artist. Closing his bakery was like Michelangelo deciding to go into real estate.

"Why are you shutting down?" I asked.

"It's not worth it. Hardly anybody buys anything anymore."

"*We* were just coming to buy something," Scott said.

"Great. But where have you been? You know how much stuff I sold last week? Two donuts, three cookies, and a bear claw. I can't survive on that."

"So what are you gonna do?" Scott asked.

"I don't know."

"You can't leave!" I shouted, sounding more desperate than I meant to. "Maybe it was just a slow week. People'll be back."

"I can't wait for that. I'm wasting too much good food."

"Okay, okay. You can go for a while. Then everybody will miss you, and you can come back."

"Maybe." And with a look that seemed to say, "I'm going to France to find people who appreciate my talents," he left.

"I don't understand," Roberto said. "He had good donuts, but his business is over?"

"I don't understand it either, Roberto," I said. I looked at Scott. "I'm gonna miss the bear claws. Did you ever try those? They were incredible."

"Nope. Never tried one. I never bought *anything* from the bakery."

"Why not?"

"I don't have any money."

I didn't want Roberto to get the impression that life was tough for citizens of Kidsboro. He had just met someone whose business had tanked, and another person who was broke.

But it was true. Scott had never earned a single token with his detective agency in the two months of Kidsboro's existence. Of course, there hadn't been much need for a private investigator.

Like every other citizen of Kidsboro, Scott had been given enough tokens to start off with. He had probably already used that up-front money and never made any more.

I wondered if this was true of more people in Kidsboro. Citizens were responsible for making their own living in whatever ways they wanted. As mayor, I was paid by the city. This meant that every month the residents paid 10 percent of their income for taxes. This money went to pay me,

Alice, and Corey, the garbage man. Tax money also went to build special buildings, like the meeting hall. So far, I had not had to worry about making a living.

Alice, in addition to being the police chief, was also in charge of collecting taxes. She was an obvious choice because no one would dare try to cheat her for fear of their very lives. Alice took care of all of this herself, so I didn't know how much anyone made at all. Were there a lot of people out there not making any money? Was that the reason Sid was going out of business?

We dropped Roberto off at his clubhouse and left him there to consider what his place would be in Kidsboro.

● ● ●

The next night there was a buzz in the air about some kind of meeting or rally that was taking place at the meeting hall. I figured I should check it out. When I got there, the place was packed.

Valerie stepped to the front and stood behind a music stand. Oh, no. It was Valerie's rally. I bit my lip to keep it from quivering as she began to speak.

"Here I have the city charter," she said, holding up a 10-page booklet. "Let me read some of the rules we have in this town. 'No one is allowed to be in the city after eleven o'clock on weekends and nine o'clock on school nights.'" She flipped a page. "Here's another. 'There will be no fires or fireworks inside the city limits.'" She flipped through some more. Her eyes widened as if she saw a really offensive one. "And it goes on like this for 10 pages." She paused for dramatic effect. "Is it my imagination, or has our city council suddenly become our parents?"

Heads began nodding in approval. She continued. "These people think they can tell us how to live our lives. They don't think we have enough rules. But don't we? I mean, we have rules in school, we have rules at home, we have rules at church and on the street and in the grocery store. We're kids! Shouldn't there be a place we can go where we are free to do what we want to do?"

More and more heads were nodding. The meeting hall began to buzz with protesting murmurs. Valerie raised her fist with confidence, shouting, "We don't need the city council and the mayor to be our babysitters!"

An unidentified voice shouted, "Yeah!" and others followed with the same exclamation. Most of the crowd were sitting high up in their seats, ready for a revolt. Four people were notably *not* sitting up in their seats. Me, of course, and three other members of the city council. Alice was standing in the front corner with her hand on her hip (where a real police officer would have a gun), poised to extinguish a riot if she needed to.

Valerie was about to continue when someone ran up. "Hey, come on! There's been a break-in at Marcy's house! The new kid did it!" Everyone rushed past me to see what all the excitement was about. I was the last one out.

● ● ●

When I arrived at Marcy's, the scene was clear. She was standing in the middle of her house, looking at all of her stuff. It looked as if someone had clobbered the room with a baseball bat. No one kept anything expensive in their houses, but she had a chair, some pictures, a few books, and a clock that were destroyed. Her walls were cracked in several places as well.

"Are you okay?" I asked her.

Her mouth was open in disbelief. "Yeah. Why would anybody do this?"

"I don't know," was all I could say.

Roberto was there too. Alice grabbed him and started searching him, just in case he was actually carrying a weapon. She stood him straight up facing the outside wall of the clubhouse, bending his arm across his lower back, and read him his rights (which she'd memorized for just such an occasion as this).

I went up to her. "What happened?"

"Marcy came home, and the door was wide open. The whole place was trashed. When I got here, this little punk was still standing here like the cat that ate the canary," Alice said, bending his arm farther toward his head. Roberto winced.

"You saw Roberto trashing your place?" I asked Marcy.

"No. But he was here. Standing right outside the door."

"Roberto, were you in Marcy's house?"

"Yes," he said, "but . . . I-I did not do it."

The crowd, all ready to hang somebody after Valerie's speech, didn't believe him. Alice took Roberto away and put him in the town jail.

THREE

ROBERTO TAKES THE FALL

THE CITY CHARTER STATES THAT if anyone is arrested, he or she must go to jail until an investigation can be completed. This was the first time in Kidsboro's short history that we had to use this page of the city charter.

Alice would do the investigation, Roberto would be put on trial, and then if he were found guilty, the jury would have to decide what the punishment should be. If Roberto were convicted, there would be no other choice for us but to kick him out of town. This was a serious crime.

Scott started to argue with Alice about who should do the investigation, but Alice put a stop to that right away. "Are you a member of the police force?" she asked, pushing up her sleeves.

"No," Scott said.

"Well, this is official police business."

"I'm a private investigator. I can investigate for you."

"If a private citizen hires you, you can investigate. Until then, this is a crime scene. Get back."

Scott backed off without another word. This was the first

real police work Alice had had the opportunity to do. No way was anybody going to move in on it.

Alice looked over the crime scene, took statements from Marcy and Roberto, and checked around to see if there were any other witnesses.

There weren't. Things didn't look too good for Roberto. In fact . . . I was beginning to think he might actually have done it. I wanted to believe him, but frankly, all the evidence pointed in his direction. I went to the jail to talk to him.

● ● ●

Roberto was obediently sitting in the cell, which was barely larger than a closet. The bars were made out of thin tree branches, and anybody with the strength of a kitten could get out, but the understanding was that you wouldn't try. I guess all of our rules were pretty much this type of understanding.

Roberto barely looked up when I walked in. He acted like a guy who'd just missed a million-dollar free throw. Being a part of Kidsboro was his chance to fit in somewhere, and it looked like it was slipping away.

I sat at Alice's desk outside the cell and looked into his eyes. He stared back at me blankly. I decided to be up front. "Did you do it?"

"No," he said sincerely. He explained in his accent, "I was in my house putting pictures on my walls. Then I heard someone call me. So I went to see who, and I saw this girl Marcy's door was open. I thought that maybe the voice came from inside. So I went in and saw the whole place was torn up. Then I turned around and Marcy was there watching me.

She yelled. I did not know what to do. Then that big police girl came and pushed me up against the wall."

"You said you heard somebody call out your name. Was it a boy's voice or a girl's voice?"

"Boy."

"Did you recognize it?"

"No."

"Did you tell Alice all of this?"

"Yes, but I do not think she believed me." He looked at me sadly and asked, "Do *you* believe me, Ryan?"

It suddenly occurred to me that my opinion might be important to him. Maybe I was the only person who had ever given him a chance. Now my answer to this question would do one of two things: show me to be a true friend, or lump me in with all of the other kids who distrusted him because of his father's reputation. Maybe the way I answered this was more important to him than being a part of the city. "Yes, I believe you," I said. I think I meant it, but to be honest, I'm not sure.

● ● ●

I was on my way to ask Alice about the investigation when I saw a crowd of people gathered around Jill. She was holding up a newspaper and everyone around her was waving their money to get one. "Special edition! Five tokens a copy! Read all about the Kidsboro Burglar!"

The normal price for an issue of the paper was three tokens. This was the biggest story ever to hit Kidsboro, so five tokens was probably a bargain. Unfortunately for Jill, there was not a lot of news to report in a town of 30—especially when the crime rate, before now, was basically zero. A donut had been stolen from Sid's Bakery a couple of months earlier and Jill had had a field day with that. It was front-page news for three issues. She did extensive interviews, took photographs of the crime scene, wrote feature stories on the history of the bakery and the history of donuts and the history of stolen donuts—and then Sid remembered that he had eaten the donut. Jill had got a lot of ribbing for that. I was sure that she wanted to save face now with this new story.

I went up to Jill and took five tokens out of my pocket. "How did you do this so fast?"

"Ryan, dear, old news is no news. And this is the biggest story in the history of Kidsboro."

"Yeah, but how did you get all the information already?"

"You wanna know what made the front page of my last issue? Alice's new police badge that she bought at a carnival," she said, rolling her eyes. "Let's just say I was inspired."

I smiled and looked at the story. She had certainly made headway in the last two hours. She had summaries, interviews, pictures of the scene (apparently she'd gone to a one-hour photo place), biographies of all the people involved . . . Wait a minute!

My face turned hot as I flipped to page two of the story. Jill had made her way down the street and was giving change to someone. I stormed over to her.

"What is this?" I shook the paper.

"What?" she asked innocently.

"You mentioned that Roberto's father is in jail!"

"Yeah."

"First of all, that's a rumor. Second, how dare you *print* it!"

"It's a fact related to the story."

"It has nothing to do with the story."

"Don't you think it's important?"

"No, I don't!" I shouted. "It has nothing to do with whether he broke into Marcy's house!"

"He did it, Ryan. Everybody knows it."

"*I* don't know it. In fact, I'm beginning to doubt that he had anything to do with it. The point is, he hasn't had a trial yet. He's innocent until proven guilty in court."

She breathed heavily a few times, then realized she had no comeback.

"Don't tell me how to do my job." She charged off.

● ● ●

The trial process was a little sketchy, but it was outlined in the city charter. There were three lawyers in town. One was Pete Marvison, whose only qualifications were that he liked the idea of being a lawyer and watched a lot of lawyer television shows. Pete was Roberto's lawyer.

Pete was smart enough, and I didn't doubt that he might actually make a good lawyer. The problem was that his opponent was none other than Valerie Swanson. Valerie could make anyone look dumb, and Pete knew it. He knew he would be no match for her, and everyone could tell he was more than a bit nervous about opposing her.

Pete came into the courtroom with a huge stack of disorganized papers, and, of course, as soon as he stepped through the door, he dropped all of them. He fell to his knees and scrambled to retrieve them before too many people noticed.

I knew Pete was really in trouble when he shouted, "Objection!" before the trial even started. Amy, the judge, said, "What are you objecting to?" and Pete slid back down in his chair and sheepishly answered, "Never mind."

Valerie spoke well. She used big words and concepts like "reasonable doubt." She even threw in some Latin at one point, and I could tell this made an impression on the jury. Her first witness was Officer Alice. Alice obviously thought Roberto did it. Later on, Valerie had the nerve to mention Roberto's father. I glanced at Pete, hoping for an objection, but he was sitting in his chair, trying to get chocolate off of his sleeve.

Pete asked Alice a few questions too, but they were completely beside the point. He asked her if she really thought girls could be police officers. Alice, and pretty much everyone else in the room, was offended by this question. Alice rolled up her sleeves like she was going to deck him, but before she could, Pete quickly said, "No further questions, Your Honor," and backed away.

The five-person jury went outside to discuss the case, but everyone knew the verdict was already decided. They returned in 30 seconds to declare Roberto guilty. And just as I had figured, the punishment was banishment from the town.

● ● ●

After the trial, I stepped over to the defense table. Roberto had his head in his hands.

"I'm sorry," was all I could say.

He stood up. He wouldn't look me in the eye.

"Hey," I said. "We're still friends, okay?"

He thought for a second, chuckled, then said, "Were we friends before?"

"We will be now."

I don't think he believed me, but he managed a smile anyway. "Yes. I'm sure we will." I think he assumed that I would never talk to him again.

● ● ●

I was hoping to look further into the crime, but I felt like I had to get on with some mayoral duties first. I had several appointments with Kidsboro citizens who I thought might be in the same predicament Scott was in—they were broke.

The first appointment was with a boy named James—a puny little kid who was probably the only person in town who would lose to Scott Sanchez in a fight. He didn't even have to duck his head as he came through the door into my office. He stood in front of me, a nervous look on his face.

"Hi, James," I said, trying to set him at ease.

"Hi."

"Sit down." He sat. "I'm having meetings with a bunch of people today just to get some idea of how everything is going. How you like living here, how you like your job, whatever. I'm always trying to get new ideas for ways to improve things." He seemed to loosen up a bit and I went on. "So how *is* everything going?"

"Good."

"You like being a citizen here?"

"Sure."

"How's your job going?" He looked at me as if I had just asked him why he didn't hand in last night's homework.

"Fine."

"What is it you do again?"

"I'm a doctor." This was the scariest thing I think I ever heard.

"Really? And have you . . . treated anyone?"

"No," he answered and I breathed a subtle sigh of relief. "You know, I only do first aid anyway. No surgery or anything."

"Of course."

"I figured since we're in the woods, somebody might get hurt. So I got this medical kit at the store. It's got bandages, antiseptic, stuff like that. And I took a CPR course, too. I'm pretty good at it."

"Congratulations."

"But nobody trusts me. A few people have gotten hurt, but they won't let me put anything on it, not even a Band-Aid. You remember when Max fell out of that tree and hurt his ankle?"

"Right."

"I went over and tried to help him, but he wouldn't let me. He called me a quack and limped home."

"So, you've never actually used any of your medical skills?"

"Just on the dummies at school."

"Then you've never made any money since you've been here."

"No."

"No side jobs?"

"No."

"So, you've never *bought* anything in town?"

"At first, with the money I had left over after I bought my house. But not for a couple of months."

"Hmm." I tapped my lips with my pencil. "Okay, James, that's all I need. If you ever have any suggestions for making the town better, just let me know, okay?"

"Sure." He turned around and left.

I wanted to think that James was not the norm. James was, after all, known for being a pretty lazy person. Surely the others would be vital participants in the town's economy.

I was wrong. All of the interviews were the same. I talked to 10 people, and eight of them had never made any money in two months. I had to do something about this.

● ● ●

I told the city council what was going on, and they agreed we needed to make sure that everyone had a legitimate job. I proposed that we establish a law where every person had to find some way to make at least 10 tokens a week. Those who failed to do so three weeks in a row would lose their houses for a month. I thought this was tough, but fair. I called it the Everybody Works program.

Making 10 tokens a week should be a cakewalk. All these

people needed was incentive. I knew that every citizen of Kidsboro had enough creativity and intelligence to come up with ways to make money. But until now, there had never been anything there to push them to do so. This program would force them to think for themselves and become productive members of society.

After some tough discussion, the city council voted four to one that we enforce this law for the good of the people, so that what had happened to Sid wouldn't happen to others. Scott voted against it, undoubtedly because this meant he would have to find a way to make some money himself. Scott needed a kick in the pants more than anyone.

I left the meeting feeling as though I had accomplished something. The Everybody Works program seemed like a good long-term idea, even if it wouldn't win me any popularity contests at first. I was working for the good of the city, so popularity was not my top priority.

● ● ●

A couple of days later I headed to my clubhouse office. Valerie and a few others were gathered out front in what looked like a press conference. Jill was there, writing down everything Valerie said. The others were listening intently.

"I don't know about anyone else," Valerie said, "but I'm embarrassed for our mayor. What is this Everybody Works program? Now he's *forcing* us to work? Don't we work enough at school and at home without having to worry about the daily grind in Kidsboro? This guy is in love with rules. And another thing, he selected Roberto to be a member of our community, and not two days after he was voted in, Roberto committed the biggest crime ever in Kidsboro. I'm beginning to think the mayor doesn't really know what's best for the city anymore."

Valerie spotted me as I walked up. She smiled that evil smile of hers. "Well, hello, Mr. Mayor." Jill stopped writing and looked up at me as well. I guessed she was still mad at me because she smiled her own version of an evil smile. She obviously planned on printing Valerie's every word in the next issue.

Valerie continued the press conference. "Like I was saying, I'm beginning to lose my trust in a mayor who votes to put criminals on our streets. . . ."

I turned away, realizing that her vision to destroy me was only just beginning.

Suddenly, it dawned on me. Of course! Valerie wanted to disgrace me in front of the whole town. What better way to do it than to disgrace one of the people I had chosen to join the town! Valerie set Roberto up! I stepped into my office. The investigation was reopened!

SUPER SLEUTHS

Officer Alice had already declared that the investigation was over, so I couldn't ask her for help. I decided to go to the Scott Sanchez Detective Agency. I realized Scott had never actually done any detective work before, but another set of eyes and brains wouldn't hurt, no matter how untrained the eyes and brains were. Plus, I had promised Scott after we passed the new law that I would help him find work. Keeping my promises—what a great elected official I was!

When I walked through his doorway, Scott was sitting in a lawn chair reading a comic book. It never even occurred to him that I might be a client. "Hey," he said. "What's up?"

"I'm here to hire you," I said.

"You what?"

"I want to hire you."

"Pardon me for being dense, but I don't follow."

"Aren't you a detective?" I asked.

"Sure."

"I need a detective."

He dropped the comic book as if his hands had suddenly

gone numb. He acted like he had no idea what to do at this point. Should he ask a bunch of questions? Should he get his magnifying glass?

"How much do you charge?" I asked as I pulled a few starbills out of my pocket. Scott seemed clueless.

"How much? Um . . . I don't know. I—I used to have this written down somewhere. Hold on." He began to rummage through a shelf. It was filled with comic books, cereal box tops, and a paddleball game. You know—important detective equipment. He stopped looking and faced me again. "I'll tell you what. Since you're a friend, I'll forget the rates and give you a discount."

"Sounds fair," I said, knowing he was winging it.

"How about half a starbill an hour?"

This rate was a little steep, but I thought I'd give him a break.

"It's a deal."

"Great. Okay." He nervously looked around, probably hoping by some miracle that there might be something lying around his office that would tell him where to start.

"Listen," I said as he continued to search. "I don't think Roberto broke into Marcy's house. I think we should reopen the investigation."

"Here it is," he said triumphantly. He held up a plaid hat, like the one Sherlock Holmes wore. He returned to his shelf. I hoped that he wasn't searching for a pipe.

"Great. Did you hear me?"

"Yes. Marcy's house. Who do you think did it?"

"I have my suspicions, but I'd rather not say right now."

"Okay," he said. I waited for him to suggest a course of action, but I was torn. I wanted to give him the chance to lead the investigation, but at the same time, he was charging me half a starbill an hour for this. I wanted to get started on it.

"Why don't we go to Roberto's old house?" I said finally.

"Good idea." He started out the door.

"Um," I said, "are you going to wear that hat?"

He stopped and thought about it. "You don't like the hat?"

"It's just . . . a little . . . goofy."

He seemed offended and, for the first time, showed me who was boss here. "I'm leading this investigation, thank you. Come on."

● ● ●

Roberto's house had been left just as it was when the burglary took place. He hadn't come back for any of his stuff. He probably didn't want to risk running into anyone and having to explain himself. There were magazine pictures scattered all around.

"Wait a minute," I said. "He told me he was putting up pictures when he heard someone call his name."

"That looks possible," Scott said. "Some of these pictures are tacked up, some aren't." This was obvious to both of us, but since I was paying him, I guess he felt he ought to observe something.

We continued looking around, but we were interrupted

by a ruckus outside. Several people were running past the door. "What's going on?" I asked one of them.

"There's been another break-in!"

● ● ●

It was Nelson Swanson's house. The place was littered with blueprints, ideas, sketches, and a number of different gadgets that Nelson had invented. It looked as if someone had trashed it just for the sake of trashing it.

"Did anybody see anything?" I asked Alice.

"No," Alice replied, having a little trouble concentrating on my question because she was staring at Scott's hat. "Nelson said that nothing was stolen."

"Why would somebody go to all the trouble to break in, trash the whole place, and not steal anything?"

"I don't know." She raised her eyebrows as if she *did* know. "Revenge, maybe?"

"You think it was Roberto?" Scott asked.

She lowered her voice. Scott, who was listening up to this point, backed away as if he sensed he wasn't invited to the conversation. "This place was wired with an alarm—and whoever did this managed to do it without setting it off. This is the work of a professional. He knew what he was doing. And Roberto's father being who he is . . ."

"I don't want to hear any more," I interrupted. She was jumping to a wild conclusion, and she knew it.

"Where's Nelson?" I asked.

"Outside. I was just about to ask him some more questions," she said. We followed her out.

Nelson was sitting by a tree, looking troubled and holding a metal gadget. Eugene Meltsner was trying to console him.

"I don't believe your efforts were in vain, Nelson," Eugene was saying to him as we walked up. "The difficult work has already been accomplished, such as the intellectual labor that went into figuring out exactly how it could work."

"But I was so close," Nelson replied.

"As far as the rebuilding process is concerned, I believe it should go much faster now, since you know the basics."

"Hello, Eugene," Alice said.

"Greetings."

"You mind if I ask Nelson a few questions?"

"Not at all."

Alice looked at Nelson. "What's that you've got there?"

"A broken automatic door opener. All I had to do was adjust the sensitivity . . ."

"Is it worth anything?"

"Not much. Just the parts."

"You still haven't discovered anything missing?"

"No."

"Do you have any enemies?"

"No."

"Competitors?"

"No."

"Anyone you owe money to?"

"No."

"This alarm you installed. Did it malfunction often?"

"No. That's what's so strange. I can't understand why it didn't work."

"Neither can I," Eugene said. "It worked consistently in the trial runs."

A voice with a Southern accent came out of nowhere. "Kinda makes you wonder if *anybody's* safe, doesn't it?" I looked up and saw Max Darby. Max had moved to Odyssey from Georgia a few years ago, and hadn't even begun to lose his accent.

Max always seemed to be up to something. He wanted you to think he was your best friend—in fact, everybody's best friend—but his real best friend was himself. "I'm sorry," he said. "Am I interrupting something?"

"I was done anyway," Alice said, moving her investigation back to Nelson's house.

"You know what you need, friend?" Max said. "You need something that'll keep you high and dry when the rest of the world is floatin' down the river."

"What are you talking about?" Nelson asked. I wished he hadn't asked.

"I'm talkin' peace of mind," Max continued, "restful nights. I'm talkin' about preparin' for the future."

"Okay, sure, but . . . what *specifically* are you talking about?"

"Insurance. The one thing that'll help you out if this ever happens again."

"Max," I interrupted, "this isn't the time."

"Oh, I disagree. I think this is the perfect time."

Nelson said, "Go on."

Max knelt down next to Nelson and put his hand on his shoulder. He had him. "You'll never have to go through this again if you have Darby Insurance. Buy one of my policies at my limited-time, special-price offer, and if tragedy ever strikes again, I'll pay you enough money to fix all the damages."

By the time Max was through with him, Nelson had bought a homeowner's policy. The way it worked was that Nelson would pay Max a starbill every month, and if something ever happened to his house or furnishings again, Max would pay to replace everything. Leave it to Max to make money off a tragedy.

But, to be honest, insurance wasn't such a bad idea for Kidsboro. In fact, Marcy, with her trashed house, probably wished she'd had insurance as well. Apparently, a lot of people saw the benefits of it. Max sold five policies right there at the scene of the crime. He sold one to Scott, and he told him his hat would be insured as well. Scott was already spending the money he was going to make off of me. I didn't buy one simply on principle. I wasn't about to give my money to Max.

While Max introduced Scott to the details of his new policy, I sat under a tree and thought about the situation. The break-in just didn't make sense. If Valerie was responsible for the first break-in, why would she do this one as well? She would risk getting caught, and she had already made her point. Everyone in town thought Roberto was a crook, and that I was wrong for selecting him. She had already convinced everyone that I had poor judgment. So why would she do it again?

After the crowd had thinned around Nelson's house, Scott and I went back in to look around. Alice was off questioning other possible witnesses or suspects, and I thought it would be the perfect opportunity to do some investigating myself.

Eugene was standing in the middle of the mess, scratching his chin. The place was trashed in an unusual way, but it was hard to put my finger on what was so strange about it. I asked Scott what he thought, and, of course, he had detected nothing.

"This is very odd," Eugene began. "The alarm is still set. Not only did it not go off, I don't believe it was ever even tripped."

"But how could somebody get in here without tripping the alarm? The wires are all over the floor, on the door, around the window . . ."

"So where did they break in?" Scott joined in, probably feeling either awkward or guilty that he hadn't discovered anything yet.

Eugene scanned the floor and the walls, then his eyes stopped at the ceiling. We all looked up. He raised his arm and pushed up on the wood. It lifted easily.

"They broke in through the roof!" I exclaimed.

"Ingenious," Eugene said.

Scott looked around again. "So, they broke in through the roof, knocked over the chair, broke a few gadgets, laid these books down on the table, threw a couple of pieces of paper around . . ."

"Wait a minute!" I shouted. "That's it!"

Scott seemed pleased that his summary had helped jar something in my brain. "What?"

"These books. Look at 'em. They're laid down on the

table like somebody was getting ready to study. If someone was coming in just to make a mess, wouldn't they be thrown everywhere, on the floor, laying open? And look at this chair. It looks like it was carefully laid down on the dirt."

"Precisely!" Eugene said. "The person who vandalized this clubhouse was making extreme efforts not to trip the alarm."

"Get Nelson!" I said.

Scott left to earn some of his money and came back with Nelson.

"Nelson, were these books already lying on the desk like this?" I asked.

"No, I always put them up on the shelf. I assume the burglar did that."

"Tell me about your alarm system," I said, playing a hunch.

"Well . . . I set up wires around the room, on the walls . . ."

"Around the circumference of the window as well," Eugene added.

"And if someone bumps it, it releases a high-pitched noise. Pretty much everybody in town would be able to hear it."

"Is there any way somebody could've gotten in here and not tripped the alarm?"

"No. The alarm must have malfunctioned . . . or maybe I forgot to turn it on, I don't know."

"Impossible," Eugene said.

"What if the burglar came in through the roof?" I asked.

"Well, sure, I didn't have any wires on the ceiling, but if somebody came in here and was throwing books and stuff around, there's no way they wouldn't hit an alarm somewhere."

"But that's just it," I said. "These books are *not* thrown around. Look at this chair. It's laid down so nicely, not touching any walls, not tripping any alarms."

Nelson was beginning to see where I was going with this. Scott still didn't have a clue. "You're right," Nelson said. "So whoever broke in must've known where the alarms were set."

"Exactly," I said. "Did anyone besides you know where you put the alarms?"

"Well," Nelson began thinking. "I've had people in my house before. I suppose someone could've noticed where the wires were."

"Who?"

"Well . . . you."

Scott suddenly woke up. "You're accusing Ryan?!"

"No. I'm just trying to think who's been in here. My sister . . ." This one caused my eyebrow to raise a little.

"Didn't someone assist you with the installation?" Eugene asked.

"Oh, yeah, Nick did that."

Nick's father worked in a tool shop, and Nick knew how to build clubhouses and just about anything else.

"Nick?" I asked. "How exactly did he help you?"

"He stapled the wiring to the walls." Nelson's eyes lit up as if the mystery was solved. "He knows the whole system—where all the wires are placed, how much pressure is needed to set off the alarm—he knows everything!"

I looked at Scott. He said in perfect TV detective fashion, "I think we need to take a little trip to Nick's house."

There was a knock at the door. It was Alice.

"Nelson, I need to take an official statement . . ." she stopped suddenly when it dawned on her why Scott and I might be in the room. "What are you guys doing here?"

"We're just, um . . ." I began, not sure if I should tell her. "We're talking to Nelson."

"About what?"

"Nothing," Scott said quickly, making it obvious that we were, indeed, talking about something. Scott's face paled.

Alice looked at Scott. "Does wearing that hat mean you're doing detective work?"

"Well, I . . ."

She looked at me. "This is *my* investigation, Mr. Mayor."

"Look, Alice . . . I just have this hunch . . ."

"And you think your hunch is better than mine?" Her neck muscles tightened. Scott started to sway as if he were going to faint. "You think you can do this better than me?"

"I'm just . . ." I began. "No."

"Didn't think so. Now go do some mayoral work and let me do my job."

Scott was out of the house in about three milliseconds. I followed him.

● ● ●

On the way to Nick's house, Valerie stopped us. "Mr. Mayor, how lovely to see you," she said. Scott had taken enough ribbing about the hat and had taken it off. "And you have your little elf with you too. How nice."

"We're kind of in a hurry, Valerie. Did you want something?"

"I just wanted to invite you to my press conference. I'm holding it in the meeting hall in about 10 minutes."

"You mean you have something *else* to say to the newspaper?"

"Oh, something very important," she said with that evil smile.

"What is it?"

"I'm running for mayor."

FIVE

THE TRUTH REVEALED

I WAS VERY PROUD OF myself for not letting my mouth quiver in front of Valerie when she said she was running for mayor. I bit my lip until it hurt. But as soon as she left, I felt my face turn cold. Valerie was the most popular person at Odyssey Middle School. I wasn't even in the top 50.

Desperate, I went to Whit's End to see if we had put anything in the city charter about regular elections and I had just forgotten about it. I knew it was a slim chance, since we had only written the charter less than three months before, but I figured my only hope was that a spontaneous, midterm election was unconstitutional.

Mr. Whittaker scanned through the pages of the city charter and shook his head. "Nope. Nothing," he said.

"But we can write something in now," I said.

"I agree that there needs to be a section about a mayor's term, but you can't write it in now just because it serves you well."

"So what can I do?"

"You have to beat her, Ryan," he said. "Then, as your first

act as the newly reelected mayor, you can add a clause in the city charter about regular elections."

If the election were held that day, I thought I had a chance. Yes, Valerie was popular, but that didn't necessarily make her a good political leader, and I hoped people knew that. Not to brag, but people in the town trusted me. Besides, I was the one who had given them their start. And, with the exception of the serial burglar and Sid's Bakery closing, everything had run pretty smoothly from the beginning.

However . . . Valerie wasn't done campaigning, and something told me she was saving her best for last. She had told me she was scheduling a debate. That would be a challenge for me. She had a way with words. I knew she could manipulate people one-on-one, so I assumed she could do the same with a crowd.

One thing that would really help me win the election would be to solve this burglary case and clear Roberto's name. Then I couldn't be accused of letting criminals into the town. Linking Valerie to the break-ins would be a bonus.

I needed to focus my attention on the one person who could get me out of this jam—Nick.

● ● ●

Nick was outside in his T-shirt and overalls, busily putting on an addition to his clubhouse when Scott and I walked up. Most people had built small houses to begin with, but the ones who were making money were starting to add on. They put on extra rooms, built extra tables, added shelves, and so on. Max Darby, of course, had the biggest house in Kidsboro.

He had four rooms, including a rec room that actually had a working air hockey table. Nelson had helped him create it. They poked holes in a sheet of heavily waxed wood and put a fan underneath it so the air would come out. It worked okay, but it had taken a while to get the bugs worked out. One time the puck caught too much wind and flew off the table, smacking Joey, the town minister, in the forehead. There was a circular mark on his forehead for about a week.

Nick had knocked out part of a wall and was building a new room when we walked up. "How's it going, Nick?" I asked.

"Pretty good."

"The place is looking great," I said. And it was. Nick was a great builder. I decided not to waste any time. "Did you hear there was another break-in?"

"Yeah, I heard something," he said.

"Nelson's house."

"That's too bad," he said, not looking up from the board he was hammering.

"Burglar got right past his alarm. Can you believe that?"

"Pretty wild."

"It almost seemed like the burglar knew exactly where the alarm was set."

"Really?" he said, making a great effort not to look at me.

"Nelson said that you helped him install his alarm system."

He paused before he answered. "I don't know what you're talking about." Ah! So he denied it. Now we were getting somewhere.

"So you didn't help him with it?"

"No."

"Have you ever seen Nelson's system?"

"No."

"Have you ever been in Nelson's house?"

"No."

"Did you ever talk to Nelson at all about his alarm system?"

"No. Look, I don't care anything about Nelson. I've got nothing to do with any of this. I've been working on my house all day." Annoyed, he sent a nail all the way in with one hit.

"But—"

"Just get outta here," he interrupted. "I'm not answering any more questions."

I was satisfied with this meeting. I had obviously rattled him, and this made me pretty certain he was guilty. I was confident I could get proof somewhere along the line. I started to back away.

"Pardon me for being born, Nick, but . . . I don't believe you," Scott said suddenly. Scott hadn't uttered a word during the whole interrogation, so I was shocked that he even spoke, much less said something aggressive. Scott continued, stammering nervously, "Nelson said that you . . . he said you helped him with his alarm. So, you're saying he's lying?"

"Yeah. He's lying."

"You didn't?"

"What?"

"Help him?"

"No."

"Well . . . you see, I don't understand something. P-Pardon me for intruding, but . . ." Scott began, walking over to a roll of electrical wire that was lying on a stump, "we found this same type of wire in Nelson's house."

"You can get that wire anywhere. He probably just bought it in a store." This was a perfectly good answer, but it looked as if Nick was beginning to come unglued. For the first time, Nick stopped hammering and started paying attention to Scott. Scott must have sensed he was getting to him, because confidence entered his eyes.

"You know, you should've seen how well this alarm was placed in a hole in the wall. It looked like a professional did it. With professional tools," Scott said, holding up a staple gun. "Kind of . . . well, kind of like this one." I wanted to applaud.

Nick brushed a drop of sweat from his forehead. "Lots of people have staple guns."

"Wow, look at this," Scott said, holding up a screw. "We found these very same screws in Nelson's house."

"Ha! That's a lie!" Nick shouted. "His walls are too thick for that screw."

"But I thought you said you've never been in Nelson's house."

Bravo! Scott looked at Nick, who was breathing hard and appeared to be thinking harder.

"Well, maybe I did go in there once. I don't remember."

"So, you're saying you remember what type of wood he has for his walls, but you don't remember if you actually stepped foot in his house?"

"Okay, I've been in his house a couple of times. He's invited me in."

"So, you're friends?"

"Yeah, sure."

"But I thought you said a couple of minutes ago that you didn't care anything about Nelson."

My chin had dropped to the ground about two minutes before, but now the rest of my body was about to join it. Scott was amazing. Maybe endless hours of watching tough-guy detective shows had finally paid off for him. Scott grilled him for a while longer until Nick finally got sick of getting caught in lies and confessed to breaking into Nelson's and Marcy's houses. He also confessed to setting up Roberto. I told him that he would probably be kicked out of town for this. He acted like he didn't care.

Scott and I walked away. I felt so proud of him. Scott seemed unaware that he had just done something incredible. He casually told me that he needed to go home for dinner. But as he walked away, I spotted him putting his hat back on.

• • •

Something still bothered me, though. I couldn't understand why Nick would do it. Scott had tried to ask him about this too, but by that time Nick had had enough and wasn't about to answer any more questions. What possible reason could he have for breaking into two houses and not taking anything?

This, of course, led me back to Valerie. Did she hire him? I could understand the first break-in. She was trying to frame Roberto to make me look bad so that she could take over as mayor. But the second house made absolutely no sense. She *had* to have done it, though. Who else would have anything to gain by breaking into two houses?

Suddenly, like a message from above, I got my answer. As I was walking back to my office, I noticed Max Darby surrounded by a crowd of people. He was selling insurance. I was pretty sure this didn't happen in real life—an insurance salesman having to fight people off.

Of course! Max was getting rich because people were scared of being robbed or vandalized! *Max* had something to gain! Max must have paid Nick to break into the houses! This would explain how Nick got the money and the wood to build a huge addition to his house. That was it! It was an insurance scam!

After the crowd around Max dwindled, I approached him. "Selling a lot of policies?"

"Fourteen total," he said. "Seems to be the hot item. Change your mind about it?"

"No thanks. I'm sure glad someone is benefiting from this rash of crime."

"Oh, I'd never want to benefit from something like that."

"I'm sure you wouldn't," I said, knowing full well he would love to benefit from something like that. "I just found out who did it."

"Well, partner, I think you're a little late. Everybody else in town has known for days. It was that Roberto kid you brought in."

"No, it wasn't." I paused for effect here. I wanted to be able to read guilt in his eyes, so I watched closely as I laid the bomb on him. "Nick did it."

He didn't flinch, blink, or blush. "Really? Never woulda suspected him. Good guy, that Nick. Quiet, shy type. That's always a good type of person to sell insurance to."

I could suddenly picture Scott and his merciless grilling of Nick, and I decided to go in for the kill. "You paid him to do it."

Max smiled and chuckled a little, as if the thought had never occurred to him. I expected him to deny it, but instead he offered a much more interesting idea. "Prove it," he said.

He had me there. I could accuse him all I wanted to, but unless Nick admitted Max's involvement to me point-blank in front of witnesses, I had no case.

Max took another unexpected turn. "Now, I know you didn't mean that. You're just fishin', I know. But let's pretend for a second that I *did* commit this tragic crime. What exactly can you do about it? Kick me out of town? I know how politics work, and banishing your most valuable citizen doesn't look too good come election time."

"You think you're our most valuable citizen?"

"Where else you gonna get wood, buddy? You banish me, and you've got no future. You can't build anything. And it's not like you paid for this wood with real money. It's pretend. Which means I can take it back. I can rip apart these houses faster than they went up. And you know, it's real cute to see you acting like this is some kind of great democracy you're runnin' here, but when it comes down to it, this town is just a bunch of clubhouses in the woods. You lose me, you got nothing." He smiled again and turned away. I watched him walk quickly over to a clubhouse and knock on the door. He had insurance to sell.

SIX

FRIENDS AND FOES

I WENT BACK TO NICK'S house. He was packing up his things, figuring that he was going to be kicked out of town. We talked for a while, but he would never admit to being hired by anyone. He never denied it either. He had learned his lesson from our last interview and wouldn't answer any of my questions with anything more than a "yes" or "no." I told him I would ask the council not to banish him if he would tell me who had hired him, but he wouldn't budge. He said he wasn't a rat. This was, of course, evidence to me that there was someone he could be ratting *on*.

But I still had no real proof.

● ● ●

We held a city council meeting after school the next day. Jill, Nelson, Alice, and Scott filed in. Everyone knew why we were there—to discuss Nick's punishment. A trial wasn't necessary since he had confessed in front of two of us. After a short discussion, we voted unanimously that Nick had to be banished and Roberto would be cleared of all charges.

Alice felt quite embarrassed by the whole thing, since this meant she had put an innocent man in jail. But she didn't protest. She'd made a mistake and was ready to move on. I think she was still mad at me, though.

Before everyone got to their feet after the meeting, I made an announcement. I wanted to vote on the punishment of Max Darby.

"What?" Jill asked, speaking for the whole group.

I cleared my throat to show them I was serious, then said, "I have reason to believe Max hired Nick to break into the houses so that he could sell insurance policies."

They stared at me in disbelief. Finally, Jill was able to speak. "Do you have proof?"

"Well . . . no. But I'm pretty sure about it."

"Did he confess?"

"No."

"Well, we can't banish him just because you *think* he did it."

I was losing them. "I'm asking you to trust me."

Alice shook her head as if I were crazy. "Sorry, Ryan. No can do. Not without a trial."

That's what I wanted them to say. "What if I get him to trial? Let me tell you why I think he's guilty, and then you tell me if you think he'll lose in court."

"Wait a minute, wait a minute," Jill interrupted. "I don't wanna hear this."

"Why not?"

"I don't want you bringing him to trial. What if he's found guilty?"

I was confused by the question. "Well . . . then justice would be served."

"Would we banish him?"

"Sure, I guess."

"Then where would we get our wood?" she said. Alice and Nelson nodded in agreement.

My heart sank. I never expected anyone on my city council to place more value in wood than in justice.

"Wood?" I asked weakly.

Jill continued, "I mean, I'm for justice being served and all that, but if we banish Max, we're in deep trouble. We can't build anything. We can't add to the population. We have to think about the future of the town."

"The future of the town?" I asked, my voice raising. "What kind of future are we going to have if people like Max know they can get away with stuff like this? What happened to our laws? Who cares about the quality of our houses? What about the quality of our people?" This was a great line, and if I hadn't been trying to make a point, I would've written it down and saved it for the debate.

Jill thought for a minute, but then shook her head. "Maybe we should let this one pass. Sorry, but like it or not, we *need* Max."

"She's right," Alice said. "I hate crime, but we gotta have wood."

Nelson nodded along with her. Scott had been completely uncommitted from the moment I started talking. My mouth hung open in shock. I had nothing else to say. I turned around and left, defeated.

• • •

I talked to Roberto the next day at school and told him he was welcome to come back to town. He was hesitant, saying that he didn't feel comfortable coming back right now. I could tell it still hurt him that people had jumped to the conclusion that he was a criminal. I understood and said that I'd be back to ask him again soon.

The election was to be held on the first day of May, and I felt that the past week had been a definite victory for me. I'd been right about Roberto. My approval rating was probably up, and Valerie had lost her whole "He's letting criminals into town" argument. So even though I was disappointed in my city council, I had something to keep my head up about.

I headed over to Jill's office to see how she was planning to cover the Nick/Roberto story in the newspaper. As I approached the newspaper office, I heard two angry voices coming from inside. I rushed in to see what was going on. It was Jill and Marcy. Marcy had one hand on her hip, and with the other she was shaking a pencil in Jill's face.

"You just think you're Miss Journalism, don't you?" Marcy said, not seeing me yet.

"I'm not running your story," Jill said. "That doesn't mean I won't run other stories."

"It's a perfectly good story."

"There are finally some things going on in this town. We don't need fluff. Nobody cares about your canary." Jill glanced over at me. "Ryan, do you care about Marcy's canary?"

I'd seen Marcy's canary. It was cute. Would I throw

myself in front of a bus for Marcy's canary? No. But did I *care* about it?

"Are you gonna answer the question, Ryan?"

"Oh . . . uh . . . I don't know. Why?"

"Well, you see, Marcy's my new assistant. I'm paying her 10 tokens a week so she can keep her house."

Hey! The Everybody Works program in motion! I thought.

"So I told her to write a story," Jill continued. "Well, she came back with a story that I don't think works very well for our newspaper."

"But it's great!" Marcy said. "It could become a regular column: 'Citizens and Their Pets.' I think Nelson and Valerie have a Siamese cat."

"Great. We'll make it a double issue," Jill said sarcastically.

"This is not *The New York Times*. We're kids."

"It's lame, Marcy."

"It's not. But even if it was, so what? At least it fills up space."

"Let me explain something to you." Jill squared her shoulders as if she was about to teach her pupil something. "There are only two ways that this newspaper makes money—people subscribe to it, and people advertise in it. Okay, right now I have 11 subscribers and one advertiser—Max and his scary insurance ads. Now if any of those people decide that your canary story is too lame for them to keep spending money on this newspaper, I'm doomed. Do you understand?"

Marcy's shoulders fell. "Fine. I'm leaving. Maybe somebody'll murder me on the way home and you can have your great story." Marcy left.

Jill turned away from me and crumpled up the piece of paper in her hand. "Maybe we should rethink this Everybody Works thing. I didn't know it would cause this," she said.

"You don't think she'll work out eventually?" I asked.

"She's a really good friend . . . but she doesn't have a clue about the newspaper business."

"Then why'd you hire her?"

"I had to. She was desperate. She didn't want to lose her house, so she came to me. I couldn't turn her down. She's my friend." She sighed, but then her eyes brightened. "I want to have another city council vote on the Everybody Works law."

"We can't back out on it yet. Just give it a little time. It'll work." Little did I know that the problems between Marcy and Jill were only the tip of the iceberg.

• • •

"Everybody Works Doesn't Work," part two, occurred the next day when I ran into Pete and Nelson. Nelson was walking quickly, trying to get away from him, but Pete kept up the pace, jumping in front of Nelson to force him to make eye contact.

"But . . . how do you *feel* about the break-in?" Pete asked.

"I don't feel anything," Nelson said impatiently. "It just happened. They already caught the guy. It's over."

"But don't you feel emotional distress or anything?"

"No. Now go away." Nelson insisted. I was terribly confused by this conversation.

"What about future stress? Do you think you'll have to go into therapy because you'll never feel safe in your own home again?"

"Listen, I'm working on a spanking machine, and I won't hesitate to make you my first guinea pig."

"What's going on?" I asked.

"He's trying to get me to sue somebody. But there's nobody to sue," Nelson explained.

Pete was unmoved by my presence. "Okay, let's forget the break-in. What about your life? Has anybody discriminated against you recently? Maybe someone defamed your character?"

"I'm in middle school. Everyone defames my character."

Pete's eyes lit up. "Okay, okay. Now we're getting somewhere."

"Forget it, Pete."

I stepped in. "Look . . . there's no place for this. We can't have lawsuits against each other."

"Can I sue the government?" Pete asked.

"No."

"Well, what else am I supposed to do? I've never made any money by being a lawyer. Now with this wonderful new law you've passed, I have to find a way to make some money or I lose my house."

"There are better ways than this."

"I'm a lawyer, Ryan. I love the law." I could tell he got

that line from a TV show, as well as the next one. "If I do anything else, it's like cheating on my girlfriend."

I rolled my eyes. Pete remained undaunted and looked at Nelson. "Now are you gonna listen to me or not?"

"No."

"You're missing out on almost certain riches, my man." Pete shook his head sympathetically, and then took off to badger more potential clients. I looked sheepishly at Nelson.

"We should've seen this coming," Nelson said. "And you know what? Somebody's gonna end up suing. And if it works . . . everybody's gonna want a piece of the action. It'll be a litigation free-for-all."

Something told me Nelson was right.

EVERYBODY WORKS

I SAT IN MY OFFICE, banging a pencil against my card-table desk. History is filled with leaders who had to make tough decisions under pressure. I'm sure plenty of people asked George Washington, "Why are we crossing the Delaware? It's a dumb idea to cross the Delaware. Let's just go around the Delaware."

I picked up a pen and began to drum it against the desk as well. I knew that nobody would blame me if I decided to change my mind about the law. If I took the idea back to the city council, they'd choose to forget the Everybody Works program had ever happened. The town wasn't too thrilled with it—I knew that. But I also believed it would work over time. In a few months, when the economy had picked up, people would be telling me what a brilliant idea it was. The thought passed through my brain that I could take back the new law, get reelected, then pass it again. But I knew that wouldn't be right. Maybe I could get reelected just on the basis of my integrity—the fact that I wouldn't take back the law, even if it meant possibly losing the election. George

Washington stuck to his guns. So would I. Maybe people would reelect me because of that.

Fat chance.

Jill burst in without knocking. I jumped when she slapped a piece of paper down on the desk in front of me.

"I'm being sued!"

"What?"

"Yesterday's paper had an interview with Corey Hawkins." Corey was the neighborhood garbage collector. "You know how Corey wants to start having recycling bins in town?"

"Right."

"So I let Marcy do the interview. And she writes in the article that after he picks up our garbage, he uses some of it to decorate his room."

"What?"

"Exactly what I said. I asked her, 'Are you sure he told you that he decorates his room with garbage?' I asked her that three times. She swore up and down that's what he said. So I did what you told me to do—I figured I would give her a shot. I ran the story. Well . . . as it turns out, Corey doesn't decorate his room with garbage. He simply *knows* someone who decorates his room with things that other people would *consider* garbage."

"That's a pretty bad misquote."

"Apparently Corey's the laughingstock of the town now. He told me that one kid gave him a moldy donut and a nail and asked him if he wanted to hang it up on his wall."

"So he's suing for libel."

"And he's got a case."

"For how much?

"Thirty starbills. I don't have it."

"I can't believe this."

"Do I have the authority to call a city council meeting?" she asked without hesitation. She had obviously already given this some thought.

"I'll talk to Corey. I'll ask him not to sue."

"That's not the point. This program isn't working. It's making people too desperate for money."

I leaned back in my chair. She had a point. "I'll look into it." She gave me a long, hard stare, nodded her head, and left without another word.

● ● ●

It was time for some more appointments. When in doubt, make an appointment. I needed to find out if this program was working at all. So I spoke to all the people who had been "forced" to get jobs, 10 in all, and they agreed to meet with me in my office to discuss their progress. It had been two weeks since I had set up the Everybody Works program, so if anyone was having trouble finding work, this was his or her last week to come up with something.

I thought I'd begin with the one person who I knew would have the biggest problem with the new law—James the doctor. It's rumored that one summer he faked sunstroke to get out of mowing the lawn. He'd looked it up in some medical journal and acted out the exact symptoms. Then after his father finished the lawn, he faked a miraculous recovery. He was actually admired for how good he was at being lazy. If anyone was going to fail at finding work, it was James. That is, unless he was pushing people down cliffs so he could give them medical attention and charge them afterward. The way things were going, that sort of thing didn't appear to be beyond the people of this town.

James came in with a much different look on his face than when he had come in before. He actually seemed excited to talk to me. Of course, the cliff theory immediately came to mind.

"So, James, how are you doing?"

"Great. Thanks."

"Are you finding any work?"

"Sure."

I swallowed a lump in my throat. "What kind?"

"I sold some lemonade and juice and stuff. See?" He reached into his back pocket and pulled out two starbills. My mouth fell open. "Remember how it was so hot the other day? I guess people were pretty thirsty, huh?"

"You made two starbills selling drinks?"

"And change. Sold about 40 cups."

I smiled. "You're kidding me. That's great!"

"I just thought about what you said about being a productive member of society and participating in the economy. So I figured I should do this."

"I'm impressed. I guess you're gonna keep this lemonade thing going, huh?"

"Definitely. Especially this summer."

"Well . . . I'm sorry for ever doubting you. You really

came through. I was beginning to think this new program wasn't working for anybody, but . . . at least it worked for you."

"Yeah," he said.

"Well, I'll tell you what. Go on and keep doing what you're doing. In a few weeks, I'll check on you to see if you're still making money. Okay?"

"Sounds good."

James left, and I held my chin up high. I felt like a father whose son had just hit the home run that won the game. I imagined turning to the other parents in the stands, saying, "I taught him that swing."

● ● ●

Much to my delight, most of the interviews went just as well. Out of the 10 people I talked with, only three were displeased with the new law. Five had gone out and gotten new jobs or figured out new ways to make money. A couple of them, like James, had rarely lifted a finger in their lives. But I guess with the right incentives, people can produce. I began practicing the speech I would give before the U.S. Congress in 25 years: "Ladies and Gentlemen, I have two words for you—Everybody Works . . ." (Applause.) "Thank you . . ." (More applause.) "Thank you . . ." (Standing ovation.) "Thank you . . ."

● ● ●

The first thing I did after the interviews was tell Scott, and he immediately took the wind out of my sails.

"James sold lemonade?" he asked.

"That's what he said."

"Do you believe him?"

"He had the money right there."

"But do you know for sure that's how he got it?"

"I have no proof, no. You don't think he sold lemonade?"

He picked up a pipe from the table. It wasn't a real pipe, it was a bubble pipe, but he claimed it helped him think. "That doesn't sound like James."

"I know it doesn't. That's what's so great."

"And the others. How did they get their money?"

"Different ways." I looked at him and grabbed the pipe out of his mouth. "Oh, come on. You think they're all lying?"

"Pardon me for raining on your victory parade, but it sounds suspicious," he said as he grabbed the pipe back. "I think I should investigate." I guess he figured he was on a roll, detective-wise.

"I'm not paying you."

"I know that. I'll do this one for you on the house."

I rolled my eyes. He had never liked the new law. I assumed this was his way of trying to prove it didn't work. He picked up his magnifying glass and hat.

And as he opened the door, someone started screaming.

EIGHT

BAD JUSTICE

THE SCREAMING WAS COMING FROM Jill's house, which was next to Scott's. Jill was pointing her finger in Marcy's face, and Marcy wasn't backing away. They were both yelling at the same time, listening to nothing but themselves. Others were gathering around to watch the fight, but Marcy and Jill didn't see them. All they were seeing was red.

"I never should've hired you!" Jill shouted.

"I wish I'd never asked you to!" Marcy replied.

"Fine. Then go ask Corey for a job. Start picking through our trash cans. I hear he needs a decorator for his kitchen!"

"If I'd known what a jerk you'd be for a boss, I would've done that to begin with."

"*I'm* a jerk? You've been my employee for three weeks and you may have just bankrupted us!"

"You take this dumb newspaper too seriously."

"Well, thanks to you, that might not be a problem anymore."

"I hope it does go bankrupt. At least you'll be human again."

This was too much for me to stand back and watch. I felt responsible for some of this, and the verbal zingers were getting way too personal. I stepped in. "Hey, hey. Wait a minute."

"Go away," Jill said to me.

"I'm quitting this town," Marcy said.

"Marcy—" I said.

"No, wait. I'm not quitting yet. I'm gonna stick around long enough to vote you out of office, then I'll quit." She stomped away.

Jill turned away from me and headed back into her house. I debated going in the other direction and letting her cool off, but I wanted to defend myself now. I opened the door. She was sitting at a table with her head resting on a stack of papers—the issue in which Corey was misquoted.

"Jill . . ." I whispered.

"*You're* the cause of all of this!" she shouted without looking up.

"You two will work this out."

"She was a good friend, Ryan. I slept over at her house when we were in *kindergarten*! I've *never* fought with her like that."

"That's why you'll be okay."

"Please! Let me call a city council meeting!"

"It's not the law, Jill. The program is working. We just need to work out a few of the kinks."

"You're putting the town before friendships."

"I'm not, I—"

Her head popped up as if it were attached to a spring. "Then how come I just lost one of my best friends?" She brushed her hair away from her face. Her eyes watered like she might cry, and she stared at me, waiting for an answer to this unanswerable question. She breathed in sharply. "There are things that go on outside these woods, Ryan," she said.

"I know," I replied.

"Then maybe you should stop being so much of a mayor and just be a kid." Jill laid her head back down on the stack of papers.

"I'm sorry." I didn't know what else to say, so I turned and left.

The crowd that had gathered to see the cat fight between Marcy and Jill had not yet dispersed. They all looked at me, searching for some look on my face that would tell them what had happened. Scott ran up to me.

"What's going on?" he asked.

"Nothing," I said.

"Well, hey," he began, excited. "Guess what I just saw." I looked at him as if to say, "I'm not guessing."

"I saw James going into Max's house." I failed to catch his point, and he noticed. "Come on! James and Max? They're not friends. They're not even *close*."

"Scott, would you please get to whatever point you're trying to make."

"I think Max is up to something."

"So, what's new?"

"No, I mean, with all these people suddenly making money, like James. I think Max is responsible."

"You think he's hiring them for something?"

"I don't know. But it seems possible, doesn't it?" I hated

to admit it, but this did sound like something both James and Max would do. "Let's go investigate," Scott said, leading the way.

● ● ●

I think Scott sensed that if he was going to uncover something here, he was going to have to do it primarily on his own. I did not want to find anything. I wanted James to be telling the truth.

We sneaked toward Max's house and watched from behind a tree. James was nowhere in sight. We tiptoed a little closer, making more noise than we would have if we had just walked, but that wasn't important. Scott was on the prowl. We were behind the tree closest to Max's house, and we could hear voices from inside.

"Is that James?" I whispered.

"I can't tell," Scott said. The leaves crunched under Scott's feet as he inched closer. Suddenly, the door swung open. He scurried back to the tree.

James came out of the house. "It's due Monday," Max said to him from inside. James had a thick book in his left hand.

"Okay," James replied like a servant to his king. James closed the door behind him.

"Let's get him," I whispered.

"Wait," Scott said. "Let's just follow him for a minute."

James went through the downtown area and stopped at one of the two picnic tables that made up our park. He sat down and opened the book. He pulled a pencil out of his pocket and began to work.

Scott was ready. "Okay, let's go." We pretended we were on our way to the other side of town and just happened to see our good friend James there.

"James!" Scott said with a smile pasted on his face.

"Hi."

"What are you doing?" Scott asked as he sat down across from him at the picnic table. I slid in next to Scott.

"Just a little homework."

"Oh." Scott lifted up the corner of the thick book to read the title. "Algebra. Tough stuff. Especially for a sixth grader."

James pulled the book toward him and suddenly became very interested in his homework.

"You know, Ryan, I don't know any *sixth* graders in algebra. That's a seventh grade class, isn't it?"

"I think so," I said, knowing exactly what Scott was up to and playing along.

"I'm in an advanced-placement class," James said, stuttering over every word. This was actually not that far from believable. James was definitely smart enough to be in an advanced-placement class. The problem with him was that he would be too lazy to do all the work required. I didn't believe him, and neither did Scott.

"Oh, I didn't know that. But I guess I could've just asked the algebra teachers. I have them for math. In fact, maybe I'll ask them at school tomorrow."

"Well . . ." James was thinking fast. "I'm not actually in the class. They didn't want me to be in a seventh grade class, you know, because I'm a sixth grader, but I'm doing the work at home. I have a tutor." This was very good. James seemed flustered as he closed his book. "I gotta go," he told us.

"But you just got here," Scott said.

"I know, but I just remembered something I have to do." James spun out of his seat and practically ran away from us, stumbling over a tree root as he went.

"So, what do you think?" Scott said.

I hated to admit this. "I think Max is paying him to do his homework."

"Pretty obvious."

"But that doesn't mean Max is paying *everybody*. Max doesn't have that much homework—and he's smarter than most of those kids. There's no way he'd *let* them do his homework."

"That's what investigations are for," Scott said, scratching his chin and raising his eyebrows.

At least *someone* was enjoying his job.

● ● ●

I felt obligated to go to Jill's trial, though I didn't really want to witness it. Jill didn't have much of a chance, in my opinion. Pete was the opposing lawyer, and I hoped that he would panic again like he had before. But he wasn't up against Valerie this time; Jill was defending herself. I had no idea what to expect from Pete.

Corey was suing for 30 starbills, which was a lot. Nobody in Kidsboro had 30 starbills lying around, except maybe Max, who probably had 30 starbills under his sofa cushion at home. Rumor had it that if Pete won the case, he'd get a third of the winnings. Ten starbills would be enough for him to live off of for a pretty long time.

And Jill was right when she said that Marcy may have bankrupted her. Jill didn't have 30 starbills to pay. Obviously, she'd used her father's computer and paper to create the newspaper, so she didn't actually have to cease production. But this would mean that all future profits she made at the newspaper would go to Corey for a long, long time. Jill wouldn't have anything for general expenses. She would be no better off than James the quack doctor. Plus, the newspaper was a business, and businesses were required to pay special business taxes. She would end up owing the city a lot of taxes after a while.

The jury would not be thinking about that, though. They would probably be thinking about doing something cool. Like nailing the press.

Court was called into session, and Pete made his opening statement. He basically just stated the facts—that the *Kidsboro Chronicle* had been irresponsible for printing something that was not true, and that Corey was going through public humiliation because of it.

Jill made her own opening remarks, admitting that she'd made a mistake, but that we all make mistakes. She offered to print a retraction stating that Corey did not, in fact, decorate his room with garbage.

She also questioned the amount Pete was asking for. "Thirty starbills? The paper doesn't make that in a whole year!" I noticed a couple of the people in the jury nodding their heads when she said this. Thirty starbills was too much. Jill had a good chance of getting the amount reduced to 15 or even five. Five she could handle.

Pete called his first witness. "I'd like to call Corey Hawkins to the stand." Pete and Corey had obviously rehearsed this. Corey pretended to be very upset with the way people were treating him. He was practically in tears as he told a story about how somebody glued soda cans together to form a swan and put it in his front yard. It wasn't a pretty story, but the performance was so fake that I think it turned some of the jurors off. It was looking as if Jill might have a chance.

That is, until Pete called his second witness.

"I'd like to call Marcy Watson to the stand." Marcy stepped up, ready to tell her story. The bailiff swore her in. "Marcy," Pete began, "How would you describe your relationship with Corey?"

Marcy looked surprised by the question. "My relationship?"

"Yes. Are you friends?"

"Well . . ."

"Do you like him?"

She shrugged her shoulders. "I don't know."

"Have you ever had him over for dinner? Done homework together?"

"No."

"So you're not friends."

"No. I guess not."

"Are you enemies?"

"I wouldn't say that."

There wasn't very much space for anyone to move in the meeting hall pavilion, but what room Pete did have, he made use of. He began to pace in little 12-inch circles, like a buzzard ready to feast.

"But isn't it true that in the third grade, you had a little . . . argument?"

"I don't know what you're talking about."

"An argument about a doll?" Marcy's eyes went to the floor. She knew what he was talking about.

"Marcy, didn't Corey steal your Baby Wetty doll and throw it down the sewer?"

Marcy flipped. "Are you trying to say I did this on purpose?" There was a murmur from the crowd.

"Just answer the question, please." I had a feeling Pete had been waiting to say that.

"That was years ago!"

"Answer the question."

"I forgot all about that."

"Yes or no."

"Yes, but . . ."

"And didn't you say, Marcy, and I quote, 'I'll get you back for this if it's the last thing I do'?"

"I don't remember."

"Is it possible that you said that?"

"I guess."

"No further questions."

Marcy stood up. "I didn't do this on purpose. Why would I still care about something that happened four years ago?"

The judge asked Marcy to sit down. I looked over at Jill, who had her head down.

When it was her turn, Jill called Marcy back up to the stand. She tried to make it clear that Marcy had no intention of getting back at Corey for something that had happened in the third grade. I didn't know if it was working or not.

The lawyers made their closing statements, and then left the decision to the five-person jury. After 10 minutes, it looked as though the jury would be arguing for a while, so I left. Jill was outside facing the opposite direction from Marcy. They still wouldn't speak to one another. I couldn't look at Jill as I passed her.

● ● ●

The jury came back in 45 minutes, and I honestly didn't have a clue what the verdict would be. I slid back into my seat and held my breath as one of jurors read off a slip of paper he held in his hand.

"The jury finds for the plaintiff, Corey Hawkins. For the full amount of the suit." All 30 starbills. Corey and Pete gave each other high fives while Jill immediately left the room. I ran after her.

"Jill!" I shouted. I finally caught up to her.

"Go away," she said softly.

"Jill, I'm sorry."

She stopped suddenly and I almost ran into her. She looked at me with her hands on her hips. "Thanks a lot." She took off and I didn't follow her.

NINE

FALLING APART

I WAS SITTING IN MY office, staring at the wall, when Scott came bursting in. "You gotta see this," he said, and didn't wait for me to get up.

We ran to McAlister Park, which was on the other side of Whit's End. There was a gathering of about 20 kids, some Kidsboro residents, some not. I wasn't quite sure what was happening, but Max and several of his friends were pushing five other kids (all Kidsboro residents) on the merry-go-round. The riders didn't appear to be having fun—but Max and his friends did.

"What are they doing?"

"Max and his friends have been pushing these guys on the merry-go-round for about an hour now, nonstop."

"An hour?"

"It gets worse. About 15 minutes ago, they went into phase two. They forced them to eat greasy potato chips. A full bag each."

"*Forced* them? How?"

"You tell me. Why do you think these guys owe anything to Max?"

"You think they all borrowed money from him?"

"I've got no proof. But it sure looks that way."

Scott left to go sneak around a bit. No one noticed me as I moved a little closer. The five boys on the merry-go-round were looking very green. A large piece of cardboard with writing on it was propped up near the merry-go-round. As I studied it more closely, I realized it was a sign asking for predictions on which kid would throw up first. No one had done so yet, but by the looks of the victims, that wasn't too far away. There was also another friend of Max's videotaping the entire thing and giving a play-by-play commentary.

I wondered what I should do. Since they were not within the Kidsboro city limits, there was nothing that I could do legally. I had no authority over Max. We were both just kids in a park. But there had to be another way that I could make him pay for his cruelty.

Scott ran up and handed me a piece of paper. "Look at this," he said. "I found it in James's backpack."

"What are you doing going through people's backpacks?"

"It was open."

I looked at the paper. "What is it?"

"A loan contract between James and Max. Max gave James a loan of five starbills, at 50 percent interest, compounded monthly."

I quickly did some math in my head and soon figured out that James would owe Max about 16 starbills in just three months. Max was the only person in Kidsboro who could afford to pay off 16 starbills.

"And look at this right here," Scott went on, pointing to the bottom of the page. "It says that if James doesn't make monthly payments, then Max will decide how payment will be made."

"Meaning James will have to be his slave."

"Bingo."

"Meaning he'll have to do his homework and play along with him and his friends while they put him on the vomit machine."

"Exactly."

I couldn't figure out how someone as smart as James could be so naïve. Maybe he was so desperate to hold on to his house that he temporarily lost his common sense. Max was using my program to humiliate people.

"Okay. Max can't get away with this." I stomped over to him. He was pulling a six-pack of soda out of a black box. He seemed happy to see me, which annoyed me a lot.

"Hey . . . my good friend Ryan! You're just in time. We're fixin' to go into phase three. The warm soda phase." He laughed. "Won't that be the coolest?"

"I need to talk to you about this, Max." I held up the contract. "It was in James's book bag."

"Hey! What are you doin' goin' through people's book bags?"

"It was open."

Max looked at the paper and smiled. "Oh, yeah. One of

my little goodies. What a great idea this turned out to be, huh?"

"You can't do this."

He didn't stop smiling. "I can't?"

"You can't make him pay back his loan by spinning him on a merry-go-round for an hour."

"Oh, but you know what? Strangest thing. Right here in the contract. See that? That right there says I can."

"I don't care what this lousy contract says."

His smile disappeared. "The city charter states that all legal documents are binding. This is a legal document, signed by me, James, and a certified lawyer of Kidsboro." I looked at it again. Pete's signature was at the bottom. Another person I needed to scold. "According to this *legal* document, I can charge any interest rate I want, and I can collect it however I want."

He was right. He could make these kids spin until their eyeballs faced the backs of their heads, and I couldn't do anything about it.

"How many people have you got under contract?" I asked, not wanting to know.

"Five," he said smiling. "Hey, we're going into phase three. You're welcome to stay." He took off with the warm soda.

Five. And if my memory served me correctly, that was exactly the number of people whose lives had been "saved" by the Everybody Works program.

The first thing I had to do was call a city council meeting.

Whether it looked like a political move or not, I had to recall the new law. It wasn't working, and it was threatening to destroy the town.

• • •

The city council met, and by a vote of four to one (Alice being the lone "nay"), we agreed to repeal the Everybody Works program. Everybody could go back to living in their clubhouses, while all the businesses in town went bankrupt because nobody was making any money.

I was planning to spend the rest of the day preparing for the debate, which was the next night, but when I got back to my office, I was too depressed to think about it. Maybe Max was right. This wasn't a town. It was just a bunch of clubhouses in the woods.

TEN

THE DEBATE

On April 30, I wrote down the 10 things I would least like to be doing that night. Number one was getting dragged behind a car through a field of cactuses. Debating Valerie in front of the whole town was number two, but not by much.

The election was the next day after school, and I wasn't sure if I could turn the tide in one night. In a town of only 28 people (down from 29 after we banished Nick), you can pretty much figure out who's going to win if you simply know the people. I knew I had my own vote (unless Valerie was so good in the debate that she convinced me not to vote for myself), and I knew I had Scott's. He was, after all, my best friend. After that, I had no idea if I had any more votes. Max would vote for Valerie since he obviously had no regard for me whatsoever. Alice was mad at me for humiliating her about the Roberto investigation. Jill was mad at me for ruining her life. Nelson was a possible vote. Then again, being Valerie's brother, he had to live with her wrath if he happened to be the vote that caused her to lose. I knew a few of the boys who would vote for Valerie because they were secretly in love with her. I didn't think I could count on any girls being secretly in love with *me*, but that was a possibility.

All Valerie needed was 15 votes, and I could count six or seven that she definitely already had. And, of course, I was sure she had quite a performance planned for the debates. Put Valerie on stage in front of a bunch of people and she could persuade an Eskimo to put central air conditioning in his igloo.

When I got to the meeting hall, I counted the people. A crowd of 28 including me and Valerie. This *would* have to be the event nobody missed.

I sat in front, facing the crowd. Valerie was already there, smiling at all the registered voters. She was dressed as if she was going to church, and looked quite pretty, actually. Jill sat in front with us. She'd been chosen to be the host and moderator for the event.

Valerie showed her "good sportsmanship" by coming over and shaking my hand. She smiled sweetly and said, "Good luck, Mr. Mayor." She quickly looked around the room to make sure everyone saw this "gracious" gesture, then returned to her seat.

Jill began by welcoming everyone and introducing the participants. Then she asked us both to begin with an opening statement.

Valerie stood up and gave everyone a big smile. There was a lot of applause. She stood behind a music stand in front and began. "Ladies and Gentlemen, I have decided to run for this office not because I don't respect our current mayor. Our mayor has run this town as best as he can. He has done exactly what he thinks is best for us, and for that, I respect him." I hoped I wasn't the only one who could see how phony she was. "But I also think, somewhere along the road, our mayor lost touch with the people. He *wants* to do what's best, but he no longer *knows* what's best. And I believe I *do* know. Thank you."

There was scattered applause, and then everyone looked at me. I was never told how this debate would go, so I hadn't really prepared an opening speech. I definitely didn't have anything as polished as the one I had just heard. But I stepped up to the stand.

"I also respect my opponent," I said, hoping people couldn't detect how phony *I* was. "And I respect her right to challenge me for this office. After this is over, if I'm reelected, I'll make sure regular elections are put into the city charter. But do you really think this town needs a different leader? I have always made my decisions based on what I believe will help the town prosper. If you think I have done that, I'd appreciate your vote."

Again, there was scattered applause. I looked into the crowd and spotted Nelson. He had told me that he was bringing a new invention—an applause meter—to the debate. A few people were huddled around him, looking at it. They were checking to see if Valerie's applause was louder than mine. I wondered too.

Jill went ahead with questions. Her first question was how we planned on making the city better if we were elected. Valerie, of course, started in on her "fewer rules" campaign, except she called it "more freedom to do as we choose."

"Our mayor actually tried to force people to work. His Everybody Works program should've been called, 'Everything Works, But This Program.'" Some laughter. "Of course, yesterday he repealed this law, but then again, he also knew there was an election coming up. How convenient." I figured she would use that against me. "But let's be honest, people. The economy is in shambles. Businesses are going under, and it's not because people don't want to work. It's because there are no jobs out there. As your new mayor, I will start a program that will introduce new jobs into our community. But I promise that I will never tell you that you have to work or you'll lose your house." Some applause. I could sense from the crowd that they liked this idea, and in fact, Valerie made it sound great.

When I got up, I responded to Valerie's "more freedom" thing and said that even though rules weren't something we liked, they were still something we needed. I sat down. It was obvious Valerie received more applause after this segment of the debate.

Jill then asked a question about new ideas we might have for the coming year. I decided to take on Max here.

"There are people in this town who seem to be taking advantage of the freedom they do have. I consider that a *crime*." I didn't mention any names, but everyone knew who I was talking about. By now, they had all heard about the merry-go-round incident. I detected a smile from Max in the back. "I believe we should crack down on this stuff before it gets worse and people get hurt." Little applause.

It was Valerie's turn, and she stood up confidently and smiled at me as she went to the stand, as if to say, "This is where I lock up the election."

She began. "I believe this town has a lot of potential. A lot of potential for growth and learning and for just being a place to have fun. But I don't think our current mayor realizes this potential as much as he should. I think we should be more open-minded about who we allow to become citizens of Kidsboro. We can have a *different* assortment of personalities here and, therefore, become a city of variety and new ideas." My eyebrows rose. What was she going to suggest?

"For example . . ." she started, glancing my way to make sure I was listening carefully. She had my full attention. "Luke Antonelli. I believe most of us know him." Yes, everyone knew him. He was in Rodney Rathbone's gang, "The Bones of Rath," and was one of the biggest troublemakers in our school.

"I know for a fact that he would like to become a member of this town. My question is, why shouldn't he be allowed in?"

I had a few hundred reasons, actually. I wasn't sure where she was going with this. No one in his right mind would want Luke Antonelli living next door.

She went on, "I believe that Luke has a lot to offer our town. For one thing, his father owns a swimming pool store. Luke has told me that if he were allowed to join us, he would get his father to give us a small, used pool. Now wouldn't it be nice to have a public pool in our town?"

I looked into the crowd and saw some heads nodding. I

couldn't believe this! She was promising a pool! "There are many others who can offer so much to our town. Jerry Wilmott, for instance." Jerry Wilmott! He was a three-time convicted shoplifter! She continued, "Jerry's mother works for the city and can get access to all the equipment and property within the city parks. Wouldn't it be nice to be able to go to the nearby baseball fields and play a game there any time we want—under the lights, even? As a matter of fact, I think Kidsboro could field a pretty good team," she said with a playful chuckle.

By the time she finished answering the question, Kidsboro had a paintball field, a snow-cone shop, and a recreation center that included a pool, volleyball court, and refreshment stand. I had no idea how she could deliver these things, but the crowd seemed to think that she could. They were drooling faster with every word that came out of her mouth.

By the time my turn came, there was nothing I could've said that would even get anyone's attention, much less change their vote. I pleaded with them not to allow our town to be filled with hoodlums, but they didn't seem to care. They wanted a pool.

The next day, I went to the meeting hall and cast a vote for myself. I figured it might be the only one I'd get, besides Scott's.

ELEVEN

AN UNEXPECTED MEETING

TWENTY-EIGHT VOTES IS NOT a lot to count. The polls closed at seven o'clock that night, and at five after seven we were all gathered in the meeting hall to hear the outcome. Alice counted the votes, since she was the highest ranking city employee next to me. Also, she was considered trustworthy by pretty much everyone. She read the little slips of paper and made tally marks in her notebook. After a couple of minutes, she rose and went to the front to make the announcement. Valerie and I sat in the same seats we had sat in for the debates. Alice approached the stand. She cleared her throat, and the hall went immediately silent.

"The winner, by a vote of 25 to 3, is Valerie Swanson." There was applause and whooping and hollering from some of Valerie's most loyal fans. Valerie showed very little emotion, however. She smiled and came over to me and shook my hand.

"I always keep my promises, Ryan," she said before she went to the stand to address her town. Indeed, she had kept her promise. She had promised she would take over the town . . . and now it was hers.

• • •

I was actually a little bit excited by the fact that I got one more vote than I had expected. From whom, I couldn't guess, but at least somewhere out there I had a fan I didn't know about.

For the next week, I spent very little time in Kidsboro. I cleared out my office the day of the election, but after that I pretty much stayed at home—my *real* home. Valerie seemed to have the city running pretty smoothly. I heard a rumor that she was going to put Luke Antonelli (and his pool) up for a vote soon, along with a few others.

I did make one trip to town that week. We actually have a church in Kidsboro. It's not a building, but rather an area next to the creek that runs along the edge of town. I went to real church every week with my mother. When we first came to Odyssey, we never went to church, but then we met Mr. Whittaker and he took us. I didn't like it too much at first, but over the next two years, I really began to enjoy it. I became a Christian a year after we started going.

The "preacher" of Kidsboro, a 10-year-old, African-American boy named Joey, held a service for anyone who was interested. Joey's father was the pastor of the liveliest church in Odyssey. The singing in that church could drown out a low-flying aircraft.

I'd only been to a couple of services at the Kidsboro Community Church, and there had never been more than three people in attendance, including the preacher himself.

Mr. Whittaker sometimes came to show his support, but I could tell it made Joey nervous to have him there. It would be like me making a political speech with Abraham Lincoln in attendance.

The service was about 15 minutes long. There was always a song, a short sermon, and an offering, but no one ever put anything in the offering plate. Joey was always hopeful, though. He never missed a week, either. He always had something to say.

Mr. Whittaker was already sitting down when I got there. We were the only ones there. Joey was glad to see me. He said he was sorry about the election, and that he would pray for me. Oddly enough, this was kind of nice to hear.

Joey led the three of us in a chorus of "Seek Ye First," which I knew. Mr. Whittaker knew it too. Joey wanted to try it in a round, but I told him that would be kind of weird since there were only three of us.

Joey then launched into a sermon. This day he spoke about the Ten Commandments. I knew all of them already, so I kind of sat back and let him go through the list, smiling and nodding but not getting much of anything new out of the sermon.

But then he said something that struck me. He said, "Wouldn't it be a great world if everybody followed the Ten Commandments?" How true. No stealing. No killing. No lying. None of that. The Ten Commandments—now those were some rules you didn't mess with.

I was so struck by Joey's statement that I didn't really listen to the rest of the sermon. After he was done, Joey prayed with his arms raised, then passed the offering plate. I took it and stared at it for a second. He wasn't quite sure what I was going to do with it, and neither was I. But then I reached into my pocket and took out 12 starbills—everything I owned— and placed it into the offering plate. He looked at the money as if it were the Holy Grail. I patted him on the shoulder and said, "Thanks, Joey." He was still staring at the money when I started to leave.

"Good sermon, huh?" Mr. Whittaker said.

"Yeah," I replied. We headed to Whit's End together in silence. I was considering the perfect world that Joey had described.

I'm not exactly sure why I gave everything I owned to the church. Maybe it was because the church was the last thing in Kidsboro that I felt I could have faith in.

● ● ●

The following week, right out of the blue, the impossible occurred.

I was at Whit's End with Scott on the first day of summer vacation. We had been spending a lot of time together, mostly away from Kidsboro. Without me, I guess he didn't have any reason to be there either.

"You wanna take an Imagination Station adventure?" Scott asked. The Imagination Station was Mr. Whittaker's most popular invention. It was like a time machine, where you could visit places in history and people from the Bible. I wasn't really in the mood for an adventure, but Scott got in and started pressing buttons.

"How about the Boston Tea Party? You wanna go there?"

Just then, I noticed a boy in a leather jacket glancing over at us. I couldn't see his face well, but every now and then I would look over and he would quickly turn the other direction. It was as if he was staring at me, but didn't want me to know it. I looked in at Scott.

"Oh, let's do the Lewis and Clark adventure! That's so cool!"

I tried to listen to Scott, but heard footsteps behind me. I turned.

"Jim Bowers," he said, looking at me. A lump settled in my throat.

"W-W-What?"

"You're Jim Bowers," he said.

My leg was shaking uncontrollably. "You . . . you're mistaken. My name is Ryan."

"Gimme a break, Jim. I'd know you anywhere. What, in four years you've already forgotten me? Jake Randall."

I glanced at Scott to see what his reaction to all this was. He was half concentrating on his list of adventure options and half on me. I turned toward the machine. "I don't know what you're talking about," I said.

"Don't be an idiot, I know who you are."

Scott shifted in his seat to get a square look at this kid. "Pardon me for being on Earth, but you've got the wrong person. His name is Ryan Cummings."

"Ryan Cummings?" he said with a chuckle. "Get real, Jim. Stop the game. I know it's you."

I turned around, showing a little more anger than I probably should have. "Listen, I don't know what you're talking about. My name is Ryan, and this Jim is probably somebody that just looks like me, okay? Now would you please leave us alone?" I quickly became very interested in the Imagination Station.

From behind me, I could sense he was deep in thought. "I don't know what you're doing. Maybe you think I'm mad at you or something. I'm not. I'm okay. But I'm staying here with my grandmother until the end of the summer. I'll find out what's going on." I watched him in the reflection of the computer screen inside the cockpit. He stood there for a second, then left. I exhaled.

"You know that guy?" Scott asked.

"No. Never seen him before."

I ran my fingers through my hair and took a deep breath. Jim Bowers. I hadn't heard that name in four years.

●   ●   ●

I felt bad about lying at Whit's End, but I had panicked. It was a matter of personal safety, and I didn't know what to do. One day I would have to apologize to everyone for my deception. But for now, I tried to forget about it. I had a feeling it wasn't over, though.

Reports had it that things were going great in Kidsboro. All of Valerie's friends had become citizens. Somehow she got her pool, and it was the hot spot, even though it hadn't gotten quite warm enough in Odyssey to really require a pool. The pool was three feet deep and only 15 feet in diameter, but she packed them in there like sardines. Last I heard, she was working on the volleyball court. I couldn't imagine that she wouldn't get it.

I read a lot of books in my bedroom that week. Before we had started Kidsboro, my summers had always been spent reading alone in my bedroom. I would read about 20 books a summer. So in a way, it was kind of nice to get back to that.

I would take trips into Kidsboro just to see what was going on, but I'd never spend more than a few minutes there. Nobody said a lot to me as I passed them on the streets. I guess they didn't want to disturb my grieving process—or maybe they just felt guilty for not voting for me. Whatever the case, I didn't feel much like I was a part of the community anymore. But I still had my books.

I was reading a good one when my mom told me I had a visitor. I went to the front door and looked through the screen. It was Jill. "Hey," she said softly, smiling.

"Hey," I replied the same way.

"Whatcha doin'?"

"Reading. What are *you* doing?"

She shrugged. "Just thought I'd stop by. Haven't seen you in a while."

"Yeah . . ." I looked out at the front porch swing and motioned to it. We sat down. "I haven't spent a whole lot of time in Kidsboro lately."

"I know," she said, pushing her hair away from her eyes. I was wondering if she had a point to this visit, but it didn't matter to me if she didn't. It was nice just to see her.

"Marcy and I made up," she told me. I thought there

was a slight tone of forgiveness in her voice, and I eased up a bit.

"Good."

This was not her point. She had another one. "So, have you decided that you don't want to be our friend if you can't be our mayor?" This was not the point I expected. I expected one about a thousand times less blunt. She backed off when she saw me practically swallow my own tongue. "I'm sorry. I shouldn't have said that. I know you're just . . . depressed or whatever." She looked at me deeply, like she was trying to sense what I was feeling. "You feel like you're losing your town?"

By this point, I had pretty much recovered from the first question, so I answered her. "I guess a little bit."

"Well, you're not. We miss you. And we need you."

"You need me? Why?"

"I don't know. There's just something not right about everything when you're not there."

"You mean it's a lot more fun when I'm not there," I said.

"Oh . . . Valerie's done some good things, I won't lie. The pool's a blast. She's got about a hundred other ideas, too. The place is gonna be Disneyland by the time she's through. She's even gotten a few people new jobs in the rec center she's building. But . . . it doesn't have the same . . . I don't know, *feeling* to it. We used to be such a family, you know? Well, the stuff that happened with me and Marcy kinda stunk, but still . . . deep down we were all friends, and we liked being around each other."

"And now?"

"Now . . . well, for example, Luke Antonelli's planning on moving next to Nelson. And Nelson's scared of him. He doesn't even want to live there anymore. He says he's gonna build another house somewhere else. And two of Valerie's friends had a fistfight the other day. Stuff like that never happened before. Makes me think it's because you're not around."

"I'm surprised you'd say that. I thought you'd be thrilled to have Valerie as your mayor. No lawsuits. She probably lets you print whatever you want in the paper."

"Sure, but . . . I'd rather have you."

"Really?"

She pushed her hair away from her face again and blushed a little. She looked at me. "*I* was your third vote." She cocked her head and laughed. I laughed too, because I never would've guessed that.

"Why?" I asked.

"Because you were right. I never should have printed that story about Roberto's dad. And you were right about Roberto being innocent. And even though it didn't work out the way you wanted it to, that jobs program was something you thought would be a good thing for the town. And if we had given it more time, I think it probably would have worked. You're always thinking of the town first. You're always doing whatever's right. You're the only person I know who does that. And I want somebody like that as my mayor."

"But I lost."

"Come back anyway."

I thought about it for a second, and the next logical question came to my mind. "What am I gonna do for a living?"

"I don't know. You can work with me. Be my sports editor. You won't get paid. I'm still paying off Corey. But we've got a volleyball court coming, you know."

We laughed for a second, and then decided we had other things to talk about. We sat and talked until the sun went down.

TWELVE

PLAYING WITH FIRE

I DECIDED JILL WAS RIGHT about coming back and being a productive member of society, so I went back to Kidsboro. But I still wanted to ease back into it, so I figured I would take a job in which I wouldn't have to do any work. The perfect job immediately came to mind. I would work for the Scott Sanchez Detective Agency!

Scott was excited about having me as an employee, not just because he had his best friend with him, but because he liked the idea of being my boss. Of course, he didn't have any real orders to give me, but every now and then he would make something up. "Wipe off my magnifying glass," he would say.

I was pulling up weeds in front of the agency when I saw someone walking toward me. I couldn't believe my eyes. It was Rodney Rathbone, the biggest bully in school and a mortal enemy of mine. He had on swim trunks and had a towel draped around his neck.

"Cummings!" he said, smiling like he was my best friend. "Thought you quit this place."

"I just . . . took a vacation."

"Well, how about a little swim?" I didn't like being in the same zip code as Rodney, much less a place that introduced the possibility of drowning.

"No thanks."

"Oh, come on. What, you can't swim or somethin'?"

"I can, but I'm gonna stick around here."

"Be that way then," he said and started to leave. As if he regretted missing a perfect opportunity to pound me, he flicked his towel at me and stung my legs before he was out of reach.

After he was gone, I went inside to see Scott. "What is Rodney Rathbone doing here?"

"Oh, yeah," he said. "I've been asking myself the same question. He just made it in last week."

"He's a citizen?"

"Valerie thought he could help out with getting electricity in the houses, since his Dad owns the Electric Palace store."

"He'll never pay attention to the rules here."

"He probably doesn't know there are any."

"He asked me if I wanted to go to the pool."

"Yeah," Scott said. "I don't go to the pool anymore. Valerie's friends always hog it. And they splash water in your face and dunk you and stuff."

"What about everybody else? Do they go to the pool?"

"No. All the original people kinda stay away from Valerie's friends. Pardon me for being blunt, but nobody really wants to be around them."

My heart sank. I had to go to the pool and see this for myself.

• • •

Just as Scott said, Valerie's friends were the only ones there. They seemed to be having fun, doing stunts and tricks they would never be able to do in a regular city pool with paid lifeguards. There wasn't an original member of the town in sight.

I was about to go back to Scott's place when I spotted someone out of the corner of my eye. It was Valerie, watching her friends in the pool. She looked worried, as if she knew she was losing her grip on things. She turned and saw me. We stared at each other for a second, and for the first time I found myself feeling sorry for her. I wanted to help her, if not for her sake, then for the sake of the town.

I walked over to her and we watched her friends in the pool for a few seconds. She didn't look at me, as if it were illegal for us to be talking to each other.

She finally broke the silence. "I appreciate your concern, but don't worry. I'm gonna fix this." She left quickly.

• • •

Valerie called for a meeting, and the entire town gathered for it. The meeting hall had never been this packed. If everyone crowded under the roof, it would hold about 30 people. Today there were 35. All 28 pre-Valerie members of the town, plus seven of Valerie's friends. A few people stood out from under the roof.

No one knew why the meeting was called, but everyone (except for maybe Valerie's friends) was aware that there was a problem in the town. We figured this would be Valerie's solution for it. Valerie stood up on stage and got everyone's attention. She was all smiles, as if everything was just peachy.

"Thanks, everybody, for coming. I won't keep you long, I just have one announcement. I've decided we should do something to celebrate the new era of Kidsboro." Of course, this meant the era that started when she got me out of the way. "We've had a lot of newcomers recently, and it doesn't seem like we know each other very well. I think we should have a get-together. So this Thursday, we're going to have a campfire." This was met with a few smiles. Other people exchanged looks and shrugged their shoulders as if to say, "I guess there are worse ideas."

Valerie went on. "It'll just be a time to hang out. We'll have some organized games, each of us will bring hot dogs and marshmallows . . ." Valerie's friends suddenly paid attention. Food was involved. "And at some point, we'll all introduce ourselves and get to know one another." Most of the crowd seemed to approve of the idea, and Valerie grinned. "Any questions?"

There were none, and she dismissed us.

● ● ●

I'm not sure what Valerie expected to happen at the campfire. I imagine she had dreams of people holding hands around the fire while singing "Kumbayah." Maybe Luke Antonelli and Scott Sanchez locked in an embrace of unity. I thought it was a good idea to try to bridge the gap between the two groups of people in the town, but I doubted it would actually happen. I figured I should show my support for Valerie by actually attending, at least for a little while. But I was not in the mood to bond with Rodney Rathbone.

The night was perfect. The sky was clear and the stars were bright. There was a cool breeze blowing through the woods so that when the fire started going, it would provide just the right amount of heat to make us all comfortable. Rodney had already picked the spot for the fire—a place in the middle of town. Everyone arrived with food, even the bullies, which surprised me. People had marshmallows and hot dogs and buns and potato chips and dip and soda and cookies and lots of other things. Everyone seemed to be taking this seriously. This was a great sign for Valerie, who I knew had to be nervous.

We all ate, and the groups sort of naturally separated themselves. Valerie's friends were huddled in one group on one side of the fire, away from everyone else. There was some interaction, but it was limited. At one point, I saw Luke Antonelli squeeze ketchup on Nelson Swanson's hot dog. Valerie saw it and smiled. This was quite a victory for her, I knew. She must have had a talk with Luke beforehand.

I sat next to Scott as we ate, but we talked little. We both kept a close eye on Rodney and his friends, frankly because we didn't trust them to be nice for any length of time.

Near the end of dinner, Valerie brought us all closer to the fire and suggested that we introduce ourselves. We were to say our names and what positions we held in town.

"I'm Valerie Swanson," she began, "and I'm the mayor." She chuckled artificially, obviously very proud of being able to say that.

We went around the circle. "I'm Ryan Cummings, and . . ." Everyone waited to see what I would say and how I would say it. "I work for Scott, here, at his detective agency." I tried to say that with all the dignity that I could muster, but it just didn't sound right. Rodney and his friends chuckled.

Then we got to them. "I'm Rodney Rathbone, and I'm the town drunk." This was met with hilarious laughter from his group but no one else. I could tell Valerie was bothered by it, but she put on a straight face.

"Rodney is going to take my place as one of our town lawyers," she said.

"Oh, yeah," Rodney said. "That's right. I'm doing that on the side." More laughter from his crew.

They went on. "I'm Luke Antonelli. Pool maintenance." More laughter. This was hardly a real job. Then again, neither was being Scott's assistant.

Rodney and his gang of laughing hyenas continued, each making up a position and receiving a lot of laughs for doing so.

After the introductions, Valerie suggested we all play a game. As everyone was scurrying around getting ready, Scott and I took the opportunity to leave. I had put in my appearance, showing I supported and approved of our new mayor and her harebrained . . . I mean, *good* ideas.

● ● ●

Scott and I sat in his clubhouse and talked for a while. As we did, we heard encouraging sounds from the campfire area. People were laughing and having fun. I couldn't believe it, but Valerie's idea seemed to be working. She had brought together two groups of people that I never thought could've been brought together.

"So, what if this works out?" Scott asked.

"What do you mean?"

"Will you be happy or sad?"

"I'll be happy," I replied, and meant it. "Maybe Valerie knows what's she's doing. If it works, we've all made some new friends and the town is better for it."

We sat for a little while longer, listening to the sounds coming from the campfire. Just as I was contemplating going back to the fire to get a refill of my drink, we heard a noise that didn't sound encouraging. It was a scream!

Both of us dropped our cups and ran outside. There were a few more screams as we approached the campfire. Nelson was running toward his house like he'd just seen a bear.

"What's going on?" I shouted.

"They're going crazy," was all he could say as he kept running.

We ran as fast as we could toward the campfire. Several people were backed up against a house, acting as if they were being rushed at by angry wolves. Then I saw what they were so afraid of—Rodney and Luke were holding burning sticks and poking them at people.

Rodney was waving his torch and laughing. Luke rushed at Reverend Joey and came within inches of burning his face. Everyone screamed. People were paralyzed with fear, afraid that if they attracted attention to themselves, the two boys would pick them as their next target.

"Come on, everybody! I'm not gonna hurt you. Come over here and let me show you how friendly I can be." Rodney waved his torch wildly, and sparks fell to the ground. "Come on, you can trust me."

Luke went over to a group of people and scared the daylights out of them. The rest of Rodney's crew were getting some big laughs out of this. Alice was motioning for kids to run.

"Drop your weapon!" she shouted at Rodney. He just laughed.

Valerie was standing to the side and suddenly seemed to realize she was responsible for doing something about this. She stepped forward. "Rodney, stop it! Luke! Cut it out, right now! Put down the torches!"

Rodney chuckled and said, "Uh-oh, Luke. Look out. Our mayor is telling us what to do."

Luke joined him gleefully. "Yeah, we'd better obey or she's gonna throw us in jail!"

"I mean it, you guys!"

"Oh," Rodney said, "She *means* it! Luke, I didn't know she *meant* it. I guess we'd better *mean* it too."

With that, Rodney ran toward her angrily and poked the torch close to her stomach. Everyone screamed. Valerie backed away from him, but he kept after her. I've never seen such fear in anyone's eyes as I saw in Valerie's.

"Come on, Ms. Mayor. I heard somewhere that you *liked* playing with fire."

She started backing away more quickly, but he lunged at her. Dodging the flame, she fell. He came right at her with the torch!

Without thinking, I dashed toward them. The flame was inches from her stomach. Just as Rodney turned to me, I dove at the torch, knocking it out of his hand. He jumped on top of me and we wrestled on the ground. Luke saw what was happening to his friend, dropped his torch, and ran to help. He tried to pull me away from Rodney. Scott ran over and tackled Luke, sending him sprawling to the ground.

Rodney was much stronger than me, and he had me pinned. Just as he was about to send his fist through my skull, he glanced to his right. His mouth dropped open. The fire had spread and a house was in flames!

We suddenly forgot about beating each other up. "Get off!" I yelled and pushed Rodney off of me.

"Scott!" I shouted. "Go to Whit's End! Mr. Whittaker has a fire extinguisher!" He ran to get it. "Alice, call 911!" She obeyed. "You people!" I pointed to a group of kids. "Find some buckets or something and get water out of the pool and dump it on these flames!" They all scurried off. "You guys!" I shouted at Rodney's gang. "Help me put this out!"

I frantically kicked dirt onto the fire. It had climbed all

the way up the wall of a house and was making its way along the roof.

Mr. Whittaker and Scott ran back with the fire extinguisher. Mr. Whittaker charged the burning house and sprayed. The fire died wherever he hit it, but it had spread too far already. The house was consumed by flames.

A dozen people came back with glasses, buckets, hats, and anything else that would hold water, and began to pour it on the flames. But it was like trying to stop a tidal wave with a garbage can lid.

The spray ran out of the fire extinguisher, and we had nothing left to do.

"It's too dangerous!" Whit shouted. "Everybody get out of here!" He waved his arms, signaling all of us to move away from the town. I had a fleeting thought in the back of my mind. *What if the fire spreads to Whit's End?* We watched the flames from a hundred feet away, and waited for the fire department to arrive.

The fire department got there in five minutes, but had some problems getting back into the woods, so it was 10 minutes before they were able to do anything to the flames. By that time, four houses were already consumed by fire. Whit's End was saved, but not by much.

● ● ●

We got a stern talking to from the fire department. Scott told the fire chief what had happened, and then the fire chief took Rodney and Luke aside and lectured them for a while. Besides the four houses that were burned to the ground, two others were damaged. No one was hurt, though. Everyone just wanted to go home, take a bath, fall asleep, and forget about this night.

I wanted to go home too, but on my way I saw Valerie. She was sitting on a stump, all alone. She was shivering with a blanket draped around her. She looked in the direction of the burned houses, but probably saw nothing but the memory of a flame being shoved into her face. I sat on the ground next to her.

"Are you okay?" I asked. She nodded. Just about everyone else had gone by this point, and the crickets were starting to chirp as if nothing had happened. "Maybe you oughta go home," I said. She nodded again. I guess she didn't feel much like talking. Neither did I.

"Thank you," she said suddenly, "and I'm sorry." Probably the two hardest things she'd ever had to say to anyone, and she accomplished them both in one sentence.

"That's okay," I replied.

We sat for a few more seconds, and then she began again. "I'm resigning." This shocked me, even under the circumstances. "This is your town. I'm giving it back."

"Are you sure?" I said, not knowing what else to say.

"Yes." She stood up, now ready to go home. "Are you gonna start rebuilding the houses tomorrow?"

"We'll do something tomorrow, I'm sure."

"Okay. I'll be here." Valerie started to leave.

"Valerie," I said, and she turned around. "You did some good stuff. The rec center, that's great. You did something else I didn't do. I was trying to force people into jobs that didn't exist. But you *created* jobs. I'm going to use that."

"Thanks."

"I might need you in the future. You know, to help me brainstorm ideas."

"Sure." She gave me a half-smile and left.

I got ready to leave too, but then I saw that I wasn't the last person there. Jill was looking at her house, which was one of the ones that had burned down. She was on the verge of tears as I walked over to her.

"The very first issue of the *Chronicle* was hanging up on the wall of this house," her voice trembled. "Now it's gone."

I didn't know what to say, so I just patted her on the shoulder. She didn't react.

"Come on, I'll walk you home," I said. She looked at me, and then we turned and walked toward our real homes.

"Pretty wild night, huh?" she said.

"That it was."

"I guess I'll be starting from scratch tomorrow."

"Well . . . as for your house," I said. "Don't worry about it. You've got insurance."

THIRTEEN

BACK TO THE BASICS

THE NEXT DAY I TOLD Max that he owed six people insurance money, and he informed me that he already knew this. He had to cough up about 100 starbills to pay for all of it, since his policies didn't just cover the wood, but also everything inside the houses. Some of the 100 starbills would go right back to him when people started rebuilding their houses with his wood. But he was still out a lot of money. The look on his face was all I needed to see. Justice had been served after all.

I put Max back up for another vote before the city council. I thought the others would feel, like me, that what he did to those kids on the merry-go-round was grounds for banishment. They disagreed, saying that he had a legal contract and we had to honor that. Plus . . . we needed wood.

Well, I'd given it a shot.

• • •

A week later, the town held a new election, and I was voted in unanimously. It wasn't a terribly glorious victory since there was no one opposing me, but it was sweet anyway.

Rodney and the rest of Valerie's friends told her that they weren't interested in coming back to town, so banishing them was not an issue. I'd been afraid that was going to have to be my first act as mayor.

Over the next month, we got the rec center going. We had a pool table/ping-pong table that was donated by someone's parents, and it became the featured activity there. You could also use other sports equipment in a room next to it. People who used the facility had to pay a small monthly fee, just like a real health club. The fees would help pay the salaries of any employees who worked there. James was the first employee, and he enjoyed taking care of the place. He handed out equipment and refreshments and kept the ping-pong players on a time limit. He was very happy with his new position.

The city council also voted on more government jobs. People took jobs mowing around the trees and building "streets" made out of thin pieces of plywood so that people could ride their bikes up to their houses. Under enormous pressure from people dying for a good cinnamon bun, Sid decided to reopen his business. With more people working now, he felt confident that he would have more customers. He was right.

Kidsboro suddenly seemed like a breath of fresh air.

● ● ●

One of the first things I did after I was reelected mayor was to persuade Roberto Santana to once again be a citizen of our town. And he agreed.

He moved into the same house he had before, and everyone welcomed him back. Some even apologized for accusing him of something he didn't do.

Roberto chose his job as well. He decided he wanted to work with Jill at the newspaper. I was surprised, because she had written about his father being in jail, but he told me that she had apologized to him and he had forgiven her. He didn't seem to have any hard feelings, and he really wanted to work on a newspaper.

Jill was more than happy to have Roberto on her staff, since he actually had some newspaper experience working for a school newspaper and she was running out of ideas for news. She had bought Max's extended insurance, so she was able to pay Corey back a good portion of the 30 starbills she owed him. She couldn't afford to pay Roberto much until she paid Corey off completely, but he wanted the job just the same.

At the end of the day, Roberto came into my office and told me about his first day on the job.

"I had a good time," he said. "Jill's very nice, and she let me write an article about how it feels to be a new citizen."

"Great."

"I even put a part in there about you. About how you believed in me."

"Well . . ." I blushed. "You didn't have to do that."

"I just wanted to come by and say thank you and that it's nice to be here."

"I'm glad you're with us," I said.

He started to leave, but then turned back around. "There is something that I should tell you."

"What?"

"My dad . . . he really is in jail." I felt deeply honored that he would trust me enough to tell me this. It almost made me want to share my own secret, just to show him that I trusted him as a friend too. But I didn't. I couldn't.

Instead, I looked into his eyes and said, "That doesn't matter."

He smiled and turned toward the door.

"Welcome back, Roberto," I said.

"Welcome back, Mr. Mayor."

THE END

FOCUS ON THE FAMILY®

At Focus on the Family, we work to help you really get to know Jesus and equip you to change your world for Him.

We realize the struggles you face are different from your parents' or your little brother's, so we've developed a lot of resources specifically to help you live boldly for Christ, no matter what's happening in your life.

Besides exciting novels, we have Web sites, magazines, booklets, and devotionals...all dealing with the stuff you care about.

Focus on the Family Magazines

We know you want to stay up-to-date on the latest in your world—but it's hard to find information on entertainment, trends, and relevant issues that doesn't drag you down. It's even harder to find magazines that deliver what you want and need from a Christ-honoring perspective.

That's why we created *Breakaway* (for teen guys), *Brio* (for teen girls), and *Clubhouse* (for tweens, ages 8 to 12). So, don't be left out—sign up today!

Breakaway
Teen guys
breakawaymag.com

Brio
Teen girls 13 to 15
briomag.com

Focus on the Family
Clubhouse
Tweens ages 8 to 12
clubhousemagazine.com

Weekly Radio Show
whitsend.org

Phone toll free: (800) A-FAMILY (232-6459)
In Canada, call toll free: (800) 661-9800

BP06XTN

More Great Resources
from Focus on the Family®

Adventures in Odyssey® Novels
by Paul McCusker | Three book series | Paperback
Uncover Odyssey's past—and all-new stories with your
favorite characters—in this prequel series! Ever wondered
how the Imagination Station was invented? What's the
story behind Jimmy's salvation? You'll get answers in these
exciting tales that follow the adventures of Whit and
many others. Each megabook contains four novels in one!

Passages Fiction Series
by Paul McCusker | Six book series | Paperback
Follow new friends from Odyssey as they stumble into the
land of Marus, where two moons light the night sky and
visitors from Odyssey discover strange new powers. Passages books begin in Odyssey and transport you to a fan-
tasy land, where belief in God becomes the adventure of a
lifetime. Recommended for ages 10 and up.

Growing Up Super Average
by comedian Bob Smiley and Jesse Florea | Paperback
Since first showing up in *Clubhouse* magazine, Average
Boy has given readers a funny look at all the important
stuff in life. Now *Growing Up Super Average*, with hilarious new stories, will help you laugh *and* be super average
where it matters: getting along with your friends, handling
money, knowing God, and lots more.

FOR MORE INFORMATION

 Online:
Log on to www.family.org
In Canada, log on to www.focusonthefamily.ca.

 Phone:
Call toll free: (800) A-FAMILY
In Canada, call toll free: (800) 661-9800.

BP06XP1

THE LAST CHANCE DETECTIVES ®

Their town is Ambrosia . . . their headquarters is a vintage B-17 bomber . . . and they are The Last Chance Detectives . . . four ordinary kids who team up to solve mysteries no one else can be bothered with. Now, for the first time, the three best-selling episodes in the series are available in one DVD gift set.

Request this collector's edition set by calling the number below. And see if you can crack the cases of *Mystery Lights of Navajo Mesa*, *Legend of the Desert Bigfoot*, and *Escape from Fire Lake*.

And for the latest audio exploits of The Last Chance Detectives, call that same number. Request your copy of *The Day Ambrosia Stood Still*, *Mystery of the Lost Voices*, and *Last Flight of the Dragon Lady*.